# THE
# MUTE BUTTON

## Also by Ellie Irving:

*For the Record*
*Billie Templar's War*

# THE
# MUTE BUTTON

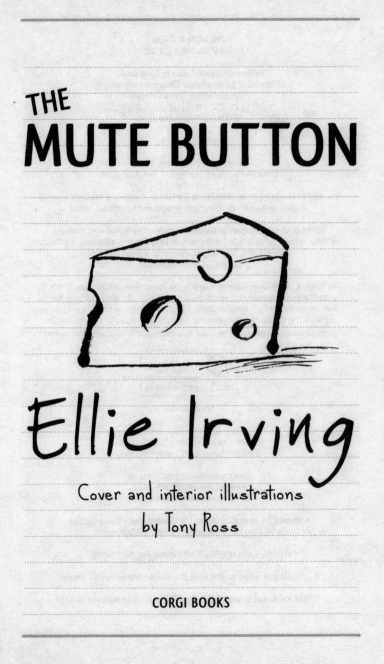

*Ellie Irving*

Cover and interior illustrations
by Tony Ross

CORGI BOOKS

THE MUTE BUTTON
A CORGI BOOK 978 0 552 56835 7

Published in Great Britain by Corgi Books,
an imprint of Random House Children's Publishers UK
A Random House Group Company

This edition published 2014

1 3 5 7 9 10 8 6 4 2

The Random House Group Limited supports the Forest Stewardship Council® (FSC®),
the leading international forest-certification organisation. Our books carrying the FSC
label are printed on FSC®-certified paper. FSC is the only forest-certification scheme
supported by the leading environmental organisations, including Greenpeace. Our
paper procurement policy can be found at www.randomhouse.co.uk/environment.

MIX
Paper from
responsible sources
FSC® C016897

Set in Bembo

Corgi Books are published by
Random House Children's Publishers UK,
61–63 Uxbridge Road, London W5 5SA

www.randomhousechildrens.co.uk
www.totallyrandombooks.co.uk
www.randomhouse.co.uk

Addresses for companies within The Random House Group Limited
can be found at: www.randomhouse.co.uk/offices.htm

THE RANDOM HOUSE GROUP Limited Reg. No. 954009

A CIP catalogue record for this book is available from the British Library.

Printed and bound in Great Britain by CPI Group (UK), Croydon, CR0 4YY

For Barnaby Wilson Rutherford, he of few words. Yet.

Name Emily
Age 9 9 months

# PERSONAL DETAILS

NAME: Anthony Button

AGE: 10 years, 2 months and 26 days old.

ADDRESS: 12 Conway Avenue, Furton Yarrow, Wiltshire a.k.a. 'Dullsville', a.k.a. 'The Zoo' POSTCODE: SN5

TELEPHONE: There's no point phoning us, 'cos Dad always answers with something stupid like 'Battersea Dogs' Home', or 'This is Bedlam, you don't have to be mad to live here, but it helps, ha ha ha.'

# MEDICAL

ALLERGIES: I'm not allergic to anything. Except my brothers and sisters. Jacob's allergic to dairy, which is ridiculous 'cos he can't have cheese. Imagine that! It's just one of the many things that's wrong with him.

BLOOD GROUP: I do have blood, yes, thank you. It's not currently in a group, though. Not like Robbie.

IN CASE OF ACCIDENT PLEASE NOTIFY: Sherlock Holmes. Accident, my foot! It'll be one of my family, trying to off me for nicking their socks, or stealing the chocolate from their Advent calendar or accidentally shutting their finger in a door when they were going on at me for being a cheesy weirdo. You mark my words.

# THURSDAY 10 JULY

## 5 p.m.

Today I am feeling like a Stinking Bishop cheese.
Make of that what you will.

If you'd asked me two days ago what it would have taken for me to start talking again, I'd have said:

- Two Xboxes. Of my own. Not to share with Robbie when he wants to play *Call of Duty*, or Susie when she wants to watch *Glee*, or Jacob when he wants to geek out on *Minecraft*.

- A trip to Disneyland. Even though I wouldn't have minded camping in Cornwall.

- A chef of my own, who'd cook me macaroni cheese and cheese on toast and cauliflower cheese and cheesecake and all things cheese all day long.

- A year's supply of Roquefort. It's a cheese.

But now. Well, now I'd talk till I'm blue in the face if it meant my family were here. Which is sort of a flaming miracle, actually, 'cos I've not spoken for fourteen whole days now. FOURTEEN DAYS! That's like an international world global record!

Still. I know they won't show up. Not after what I did.

I'm sitting on a bench on the school stage, with Samir Stamford and his imaginary friend Woody Wattler sitting next to me, looking out into the sea of mums and dads and grannies and aunts and second cousins twice removed, who are all here to see Year 5's Grand Presentation.

And everyone else's family is here, except mine.

All 'cos of this flaming journal.

This flaming journal that Dr Morley gave me, where I have to write down how I feel about stuff, if

I won't say it out loud. About what makes me angry;
what makes me want to keep on not talking.

Sheesh. Kebab.

I suppose I'd better start at the beginning then.

And I suppose, if I'm being completely
honest, it all started when Dad found out he had
another son.

# WEDNESDAY 25 JUNE

Today I am feeling like a mouldy bit of Stilton.

You know, the crusty bit round the edge that no one wants.

Seven o'clock and we're in the front room watching *Masterchef*. Well, Mum and Dad and Susie and Robbie and Jacob are watching it. I think it's the most boring show on earth. What's the point of watching someone else cook something for an hour if you don't ever get to eat it?

Mum and Dad are sitting on the sofa and Dad keeps swatting at my head with the remote control 'cos I keep ducking in front of the telly.

Let me explain about my family, in the form of a list. Mum's always making lists for stuff, writing on whatever she can get her hands on and leaving it lying around the house. Made for an interesting Christmas last year, when we all knew what we were getting 'cos she'd written her shopping list on a toilet roll in the loo.

1. Dad is called Phil. He is forty-two. He is tall and thin and doesn't like us to go on about his nose. He's a graphic designer. He likes Swindon Town FC and red wine and he says things like 'Incidentally,' and 'Can anyone remember what I came upstairs for?'

2. Mum's real name is Clare. She has short blonde hair. She didn't have any brothers or sisters growing up. She is studying to be an accountant, but that just means she'll sit at the kitchen table for an hour with her calculator and then call Jacob for help, 'cos he's a member of Mensa.

3. Robbie is fifteen and reckons he's the next will.i.am. He's sat on the other sofa by the window now, strumming his guitar. Though

to be honest, the only song he knows is 'Hall of Fame' by The Script. And I don't know why he has to play it in here. Mum and Dad converted the garage into his bedroom so he and his mates can play their music and Mrs Taylor next door can't say, 'I'm going to report you to the council for noise pollution,' again. Robbie had a growth spurt last year so he's all lanky now, and he's always bumping into things, but that's 'cos Mum says he needs to cut his fringe.

4. Susie's an actress. You can tell 'cos she's sitting on the sofa next to Robbie pretending Gregg Wallace has just told her she's made the final. She gets all the best parts in her school plays, even though she's only Year 7. Susie's the only one in our family who's got red hair — everyone else is brown, like me, Dad and Robbie, or blond like Lucy, Jacob and Mum. Though to be fair, Dad's not got much hair left. Dad always laughs because the only other person we know with red hair is the

milkman and he says, 'You know what they say about that.' (I don't, but I'm sure he'll tell me one day.)

5. Jacob's sitting on the carpet at the foot of the sofa, absorbed in a puzzle, like always. He's seven and brilliant at maths, but I've already gone over that. He has blue eyes which you can only just see behind his glasses, and he's properly scrawny and is lactose intolerant. And he plays the clarinet. So all in all he's an ideal candidate for 'Geek of the Year'. We have to share a room because we only live in a three-bedroom house (and a converted garage).

6. Then there's Badger, curled up in his basket in the corner of the room. He's our cat. He's a tabby and looks nothing like a badger 'cos he's white and brown all over, but Dad said it would be 'ironic'. *Moronic*, more like. Badger is six years old, which is forty-two in cat years, which is exactly the same age as ancient old Dad. But we're not sure if Badger's gonna

make it to his next birthday, 'cos he's a bit suicidal. He sits out in the road, and doesn't budge when cars or buses or motorbikes zoom past.

I have a BIG family.

A big family who all want to watch *Masterchef*.

'Oh my God, this means everything to me,' I say, standing in front of the telly and copying what the contestants are doing. 'I knew I could make a soufflé, but this really takes the biscuit!'

Dad waves the remote control at me again. 'Sit down, Ant.'

I let out a puff of air and head into the kitchen, where I clatter around in the cupboard, pulling out a saucepan and a colander. I'll make my own *Masterchef* dish, I think, 'cos at least then I'd get to eat it. I fill the saucepan with water and place it on the hob, then reach into the cutlery drawer and pull out the box of matches. I strike one and watch as the flames dance down the match. I let it burn, almost down to my fingers. 'Argh!' I give a little yelp 'cos it's so hot and throw the match onto the counter top.

Where it lands on a tea towel.

I watch with a mixture of horror and fascination as the match burns a hole in the corner of the tea towel, wisps of smoke rising from the counter.

At that moment, Dad strides in. 'What do you think you're doing?' He bustles to the sink and throws the smouldering tea towel in it. 'You could have set off the—'

BEEP BEEP BEEP BEEP BEEP . . .

'Who set off the fire alarm?' Mum's at the door, grabbing Susie's school jumper from the back of a kitchen chair and swatting at the ceiling. 'For heaven's sake, Anthony, you'll wake—'

'WAAAAAAAAAH WAAAAAAAAAH!'

A shrill, piercing scream rings out from upstairs. Lucy. Lucy is two and likes cuddles and watching *Peppa Pig* on TV. She always has food around her mouth. At this moment in time, she's in bed, asleep.

Least she was.

'That's all I need.' Mum shoves the jumper at Dad and heads upstairs to soothe her. 'Thanks, Ant.'

Like I said, I have a big family. A big, crazy, mad – and always mad at *me* – family.

It does my head in, truth be told.

# Thursday 26 June

*Today I am feeling like Feta. It's all Greek to me.*
*Mr Reeve's word of the day: 'Exasperated.'*

At school, I sit on Saturn table with Michael Hadley and Stacy Flack and Murphy. Murphy's my best friend, and he's properly funny. Think of the funniest person you know, then double it. Quadruple it. Times it by seventeen gazillion. He's going to be Michael McIntyre one day, mark my words.

While Mr Reeve's at the front of the class, trying to talk to us about equivalent fractions, Murphy reaches into his pocket and shows me a long piece of grass. 'It's a reed,' he whispers, and places his reed on the palm of one of his hands, clasps his hands closed like he's praying and brings them to his lips. 'Watch.'

Murphy waits for Mr Reeve to turn his back to the class. Eventually, Mr Reeve heads over to his desk in the corner of the room to pick up a marker pen, and at that moment Murphy blows loudly into his hands.

'Pffffffffft!'

A noise squeaks out – a half squelch, half farting sound.

Me and Michael Hadley giggle. 'That's properly ace,' I whisper.

As Mr Reeve heads back to the white board, Murphy blows into his hands again. 'Pfffft.' Mr Reeve looks round, but we all stare back at him with our best innocent looks.

'Let me try!' I put the reed in my hands and wait for the right moment. Mr Reeve's writing some boring old maths thing on the board, but then he takes a few steps back to look at his work. That's my chance!

'Pfffft,' I blow into my hands. 'Pffffffffffffffffffffff ffffffffffffft!'

The whole class hears it. Every table starts whispering to each other.

'That was a good one!' Murphy giggles.

I'm on a bit of a roll now, so I start blowing even harder. 'Pfffft!'

The whole class laughs at that, and I can't stop grinning 'cos it's so funny and it's me who's made everyone laugh. Me! 'Pfffft!' I time it so that whenever Mr Reeve moves his feet, it properly sounds like his shoes are squelching. 'Pffffffffft!'

But Mr Reeve happens to turn round at that very moment.

'Anthony Button!' he says, glaring at me. 'Am I going to have to separate you and Mister Murphy? Again?'

He nods to Mrs Wintour, the teaching assistant, who gets up from Mercury table and moves me over to join her. 'You'd have thought a bit of your brother's mathematical genius would have rubbed off on you,' Mrs Wintour huffs, but I don't say anything at that. So for the rest of our numeracy lesson I have to sit with boring old Jemima and Alexandra and all they do is talk about horses. Blah!

School gets better at ten past three, because that's when it finishes.

Murphy, Michael Hadley and me head over to the back of the field to play football while we wait for our mums, and Michael has to go in goal, 'cos he's not very good. Not like me. I'm quite brilliant at football, if I say so myself. Not Messi, or anything, but take today—

Mum's turned up and she's shouting at me that we're going to be late if I don't come THIS VERY SECOND, but this really mint thing happens where I ignore her and keep nudging the ball forward and I chip the ball in right over Michael's head.

'GOAL!!!!!' Murphy shouts. 'GO ON, MY SON!' He slaps me on the shoulder and I can't stop beaming.

'Anthony!' Mum calls across the field. 'Get a

move on! We can't be late for Ben.'

I let out a puff of air.

Ben. I forgot about Ben.

Ben's nineteen. He's not really my brother, or anything – he's just this guy Dad found out was his son a few weeks ago. But tonight's the night the rest of us are meeting him for the first time. We're going to Pizza Express, because Mum's got a voucher, and I already know I'm having the Padana pizza, which is Mozzarella *and* goat's cheese. It's dairy good. (That's a little cheese joke.) And it's pretty much the only good thing about all of this, if I'm honest.

# Thursday 26 June

## 6.13 p.m.

Dad's super-stressed. He's wearing a tie, which he doesn't even have to do for work and so far he's said, 'Do I look all right?' to Mum exactly nine times. Mum didn't bother replying after four.

When we get to the restaurant and Dad says, 'Reservation for Button,' the waiter takes one look at us and says, 'We're gonna need a bigger table,' which is what most people say when they see us coming, because we're a bit like a circus troupe or a small army. The waiter gets a high chair and colouring book for Lucy, but she starts eating the purple crayon while we're all eating the breadsticks.

Dad checks his watch a million times, and slicks down his hair and bites his nails. Our table is all the way at the back of the restaurant, so every now and then Dad keeps standing up because he thinks he's seen Ben.

'That's a middle-aged woman,' Mum says the first time Dad stands up.

'That's an old man,' Robbie says when Dad stands up the second time, knocking into the table and rattling all the cutlery.

'That's a pot plant,' I say the third time, because this is getting ridiculous.

Mum leans over Lucy and gives Dad's shoulder a squeeze. 'He'll be here soon enough, love,' she says, but I can tell she's just as nervous as Dad is.

Ten minutes later, we're still waiting. Jacob's taken out a Sudoku book and he's quietly working away on 'Extremely Challenging', which is like 'a Walk in the Park' for him. Robbie's drumming some beat on the table with his hands and Susie's chair-dancing next to him. I'm pulling faces at Lucy, trying to make her giggle, when I get a genius

idea to *properly* amuse her, and to make Dad laugh.
I take two breadsticks and I shove them under my
top lip.

'I'm a walrus!' I snarl, making out the breadsticks
are like fangs, and I look around the table and
everyone laughs along with me.

'God, you're such a geek,' Robbie mutters under
his breath, and he shifts his chair to make it look like
he's got nothing to do with this crazy bunch. The
corners of Dad's mouth twitch.

'And I'm so hungry, I'm going to eat you up!'
I say, and I pounce on Lucy and pretend to nibble
on her neck. Lucy screams with laughter and Mum
shushes us, but she doesn't mind too much. Then
Lucy grabs one of the breadsticks and snaps it off.
'Owwwww!' I pretend to writhe around in agony.
'That's my tooth!'

Susie clutches her mouth and contorts her face
in pain. 'You do it more like *this*, actually,' she says,
screwing up her eyes, and it properly looks like
someone's punched her in the jaw.

'Keep it down,' Dad says, though he's still looking

across the restaurant and doesn't really pay too much attention.

Lucy makes a grab for the other breadstick and I jolt back so she can't have it. But just as I'm jolting back, my arm knocks into the water jug, and before I can do anything it goes flying across the table and water spills everywhere . . .

Right over this tall man, who's standing at the edge of our table. The water splashes his trousers, runs all down his legs, and soaks the top of his belt. No one says anything for a moment. Then the tall man clears his throat.

'Um, Dad?' he says. It takes a second to work out what's going on, because this man's saying 'Um, Dad?' to *my dad*.

Dad leaps up from the table. 'Ben!' He sort of shakes himself and then opens his arms and leans in. At the same time, Ben holds out his hand and they have this awkward, half-hug, half-handshake moment.

'Nice to see you again,' he says to Dad.

Dad shakes his head at Ben's trousers. 'I'm so

sorry,' he says, and he looks at me like he's going to *slaughter* me.

Ben runs his hand through his hair and wipes his big conk of a nose. 'That's all right,' he laughs. 'I *like* looking like I've wet myself.' He shrugs his suit jacket off and places it on the back of the chair and then sits down at the table, right next to me. 'Reminds me of being seven years old, all over again.' And he flashes this big grin at all of us.

Jacob looks over at him shyly and smiles. He's found a friend there, I think, because every now and then Jacob still wets the bed. It's one of the many downsides of sharing a room. Mum's made me promise not to tell *anyone*.

Dad laughs like it's the funniest thing he's ever heard and we all look at him like he's had a frontal lobotomy. He picks up a handful of napkins from the table and thrusts them at Ben. 'Did you find it all right?' Dad asks, straightening his tie.

Ben nods and wipes the water off his trousers. I look down and notice that he's got a posh shiny silver watch on his wrist. 'I only work over at

Hunter and Sons, so it's not a million miles away,' he says.

Well, this is a barrel of laughs.

'Technically, nowhere on Earth is a million miles away,' Jacob says softly, still working on his Sudoku. 'Did you know the furthest point from the Earth's centre is Chimborazo, in Ecuador?'

Ben grins again. 'No, I didn't know that.'

Susie flips her hair back dramatically. 'No one does. He's a member of Mensa.'

Dad reaches over and ruffles Jacob's hair. 'This is Jacob,' he says to Ben by way of introduction. 'Or, as we like to call him, Einstein.'

'Or "Know-It-All", or "Stop-Banging-On",' Robbie mutters under his breath, but we all catch him.

'Yes, thank you, Robbie,' Mum pipes up. She turns to Ben and reaches out her hand. 'Clare. You'll have to excuse us, we're all a bit flustered.'

'We're *always* a bit flustered,' Susie retorts, 'but that's life, I suppose. "Like madness is the glory of this life, as this pomp shows to a little oil and root." William Shakespeare.'

Dad's practically glowing with pride. 'Susie's always the star of the show,' he says, pouring Ben a glass of wine and helping himself to a second. 'Gets all the best parts in the school plays.'

Susie waves her hand at Dad like she's dead embarrassed but I can tell she's loving it.

'And Robbie's a regular Jimi Hendrix,' Dad carries on, beaming at Robbie.

'Oh, yeah?' Ben says, looking impressed. 'What sort of bands do you like?'

Robbie shrugs and pushes his fringe out of his eyes.

Ben reaches into his suit jacket and takes out an iPod. 'You heard of The Maccabees?' He leans across the table to give Robbie the iPod but Lucy gets there first.

'No,' Mum says gently, loosening her grip on it. 'Lucy, give it to Robbie.'

'She's starting young,' Ben laughs, and he and Mum share a smile as Mum passes the iPod to Robbie, and before I can even say, '*I've* never heard of The Maccabees,' Robbie's got his earbuds in, his eyes shut and he's nodding away like he's their biggest fan.

Then I remember the brilliant thing that happened today! Not the whole Mr-Reeve-squelching-shoes thing, 'cos I don't reckon Dad would appreciate that – Murphy says you have to 'know your audience' – but the goal! My brilliant goal this afternoon!

But just as I'm about to say, 'Hey, guess what I did?' Dad winks at Ben. 'What about you then, Ben? What are you interested in?'

Ben smiles. 'I quite like a kick-about,' he replies.

Oh, do you now? I think. Bet you didn't score an ace goal this afternoon, did you?

'I'm no van Persie,' Ben laughs, 'but I'm not bad.'

Dad claps his hands together. 'I knew it! Let me guess, you support Swindon!'

Ben shakes his head ruefully. 'Bristol Rovers.'

'What?!' Dad booms, acting like he's mortally offended. I can see where Susie gets it from. 'How did this happen?'

The two of them smile at each other, and Dad lifts his glass in a toast. 'To family.' His eyes water, like he's got a bit of grit in them, and he gulps back his glass of wine.

I'm bored of this conversation already, so I take the little candle that's been placed on our table and wave the small packet of butter from my side plate over it. After a minute or two it melts, and gooey gold butter drips out of the packet onto the tablecloth in front of me. I try and make a pattern out of it, like the swirly carpet in our front room.

'I would have liked to have a kick-about with you, in the park or something,' Dad says to Ben quietly. 'You know, when you were growing up.'

Ben takes a deep breath, and smiles. 'We still can.'

Hang on a second, I think. What with Dad working all hours to feed and clothe us and pay all the bills, he's hardly got any time for football with *me*.

Ben shifts in his seat. 'What about you, then?' he says, peering down on me. 'What's your skill?'

Dad smacks his hand to his head. Mum frowns at him, like she thinks he's had a bit too much wine. 'I forgot about you!' Dad grins.

Well, thanks very much.

'This is Anthony,' Dad booms. 'He's – well, he—Anthony? What do you like?'

I mean, what can I say?

'Oh, *now* he stops talking,' Dad says, rolling his eyes at Ben. 'Normally you can't shut him up.'

Ben smiles at me expectantly. Well, I can't tell everyone about my ace goal now that Ben's banged on about football, 'cos it'll just look like I'm copying, and I can't play guitar, and I'm a rubbish actor and I don't much like Sudoku.

'I like cheese,' I say eventually.

Everyone bursts out laughing at that. 'What?' I mumble. 'I do! I can name over four hundred and three different varieties.'

Ben claps his hand to his mouth, his shoulders shaking. 'Well, I'll *Brie* damned,' he says, trying to look solemn.

Dad's bottom lip wobbles. 'You'd Cheddar believe it,' he snorts.

Susie holds her hand to her forehead and pretends to faint. 'Frankly, my dear, I don't give Edam.'

She giggles so loudly that Robbie takes out his ear-buds. 'That's a Gouda one,' he smirks.

'Yes, very mature,' I snap, but that just makes everyone laugh even more. 'What?'

Jacob looks at me over his puzzle book. 'Mature,' he whispers, 'like cheese.'

I frown and fold my arms.

Then the waiter comes to take our order and now I don't feel like having the cheese pizza. I end up going for a pepperoni and when it comes it's so hot I burn the roof of my mouth.

I suppose this is what gives me the idea.

It's during dessert, and Ben and Dad are getting on like a house on fire. Robbie's happy because Mum let him have half a glass of wine, seeing as it's a special occasion. Lucy's finished her chocolate cake, though most of it's smeared around her mouth, and she's making a grab for my dessert, and 'cos I'm still annoyed at everyone laughing at me, I felt I couldn't have my usual cheeseboard, so had to go for the Toffee Fudge Glory instead, though it's not particularly glorious.

I push my plate away so Lucy can't reach it, because she has a habit of smearing food not just around *her* mouth but all over *your* face and cheeks and hair and I'm properly not in the mood for that, so I try telling her off, but she doesn't really pay attention.

I turn to Mum to tell her, but she's having an argument with Susie, who's kicking off because Mum won't let her have any wine, even though she's twelve, which is practically eighteen. So I hold my fork away from Lucy, except I accidentally jab it in Jacob's forehead, and as well as Toffee Fudge Glory he's got four little prong marks on his face and he screams out in pain.

Dad looks over at me. 'What's going on?'

'Nothing, I—'

'Jacob, you're bleeding,' Ben says, taking his napkin and swatting Jacob's forehead with it.

'It's just a bit of Toffee Fudge,' I grumble, but Dad frowns at me.

Next to me, Susie's still whining at Mum. 'But I only want a sip,' she's saying.

**MUM:**   I've already said no.

**SUSIE:**   Lindsay Lohan started drinking at thirteen.

**MUM:**   That's not a viable argument.

**BEN:**   Do you need more napkins?

**JACOB:**   No, I think I'm fine. It stings, though.

**ME:**   Stop being a baby.

**DAD:**   Anthony, will you behave yourself?

**ROBBIE:**   Can you pass the wine?

**MUM:**   Don't you start.

**ME:**   I'm not even doing anything.

**MUM:**   I wasn't talking to you.

**ME:**   Why not? What have I done?

**LUCY:**   More cake.

**MUM:**   You've had enough.

**ME:**   You're not having my Toffee Fudge Glory. Robbie already got a bigger bit than me.

**ROBBIE:**   That's 'cos I'm the number one son, and you're son number two. No — three, now Ben's here.

**ME:**   Mum! Tell him!

**BEN:**   You know, I think I should be making a move.

**DAD:**   No, it's all right. Stay for a coffee.

**ME:**   Bye, then.

| | |
|---|---|
| **DAD:** | Anthony! |
| **ME:** | What? |
| **DAD:** | I've had just about enough of you this evening. |
| **ME:** | I'M NOT DOING ANYTHING! |
| **MUM:** | Shh, stop making a scene. |
| **ME:** | I'm not the one crying over a bit of cake on my forehead! |
| **SUSIE:** | Mum, you're being so unfair! |
| **JACOB:** | Has the blood gone yet? |
| **ME:** | There wasn't even any blood. |
| **DAD:** | Anthony, that's enough. Hold your tongue! |
| **BEN:** | Just a latte, maybe. |
| **ME:** | But I'm not— |
| **DAD:** | Anthony, I don't want to hear another peep from you all evening, all right? |
| **LUCY:** | I feel sick. |

So that's what gave me the idea. Fine, Dad, I think. I'll hold my tongue all right.

Things eventually calmed down around the table – Jacob stopped being such a big baby just because I'd accidentally jabbed him in the face with my fork; Lucy wasn't sick and just sat there sucking her thumb, and Dad couldn't stop pulling 'sorry about all this' faces at Ben. Ben looked a bit traumatized by everything, truth be told.

And I didn't say anything else all night. Not when it came to getting the bill and everyone squabbled over the mints that came with it; not when it came to getting our coats on and Mum saw the little puddle of butter on the tablecloth and said, 'Oh, *Anthony*,' like that; not when the waiter said, 'Oh, please come again,' though he looked like he was actually thinking, *I'm probably going to hand in my resignation if you do*, and not when it came to saying goodbye to Ben in the car park.

Robbie and Ben high-fived and Ben promised to dig out some old albums of his. Then he told Jacob he was wearing a cool top, even though it's *my* old Spider-Man top but I'm too big for it now so Jacob has to wear it. Then Ben gave Susie and Lucy a big cuddle. I didn't really feel like hugging, so I went and sat in the car. Mum gave Ben a kiss on the cheek and Dad held him in a hug that lasted at least thirteen seconds.

The whole journey back, Dad sat in the passenger seat with a big stupid grin on his face. He kept going over the evening with Mum, saying things like, 'Did you see Ben laugh when I said this?' and, 'Did you see when Ben did that?'

I felt like shouting, 'No, we all sat staring at the wall all night – of *course* we saw it!'

But I didn't say anything, still.

Not that anyone noticed. Robbie had his head slumped against the window, Jacob was looking at the atlas he keeps in the back of the car, Lucy was fast asleep and Susie was gazing wistfully at the moon, no doubt thinking about *Romeo and Juliet*.

Dad's still in a brilliant mood as we're all getting ready for bed. He pops his head round the bathroom door as I'm brushing my teeth and says, 'Night, night, Ant,' with that big stupid grin on his face, and he doesn't even wait for me to spit out my toothpaste to say goodnight back, so he didn't even see that I wasn't talking.

Hmph.

Then, when Jacob and me are in bed and Mum comes in to switch off the light, she just says a quick, 'Lights out,' then flicks the switch and goes to join Dad where he's hovering on the landing outside our room.

'Well done, love,' Mum whispers, and Dad beams like she's just told him Swindon have won the Premiership.

'I think that went rather well, didn't it?' he replies. He kisses her forehead and the two of them walk downstairs.

Well, no, actually. I *don't* think that went rather well.

Not at all.

But nobody seems to be bothered about what *I* think.

# Friday 27 June

Today I am feeling like a Bardney Blue goat's cheese.
Nobody understands me.

MR REEVE'S WORD OF THE DAY: 'EXASPERATED.' Again.

I didn't say a single word all through breakfast this morning. But breakfast is always a bit manic in our house, with Mum shouting up the stairs every two minutes for all of us to share the bathroom, Susie moaning that she can't find her science textbook, Robbie forgetting to put his PE kit in the wash and having to dab the grass stains off with a sponge, and Lucy needing help with her potty. The only one who gets out of it is Jacob, because a boy from his special school picks him up an hour earlier than everyone else.

So nobody really noticed when I didn't say anything. Sometimes I think it would take me dancing down the stairs with my underpants on my head and a bin bag taped to my back like a cape to make this family sit up and pay attention. Which actually happened once, but Mum just laughed and took a photo for the family album. Or 'future blackmail', as Dad called it.

Mr Reeve is on playground duty when we get to school and he says a friendly 'hello' to Mum and Lucy and me. But I don't say anything back, and I didn't say goodbye to Mum and Lucy and I didn't even say hello to Murphy when he came over to ask if I wanted a kick-about in the playground. But nobody asked me why.

After assembly, Mr Reeve got the other Year 5 class to join us in our classroom and he and Miss Watson, 5W's teacher, talked to us about our end-of-term assignment. It's called 'My Family and Other Animals' and everyone has to do a

*THREE-MINUTE* presentation on their family tree.

I can tell you all about my family in three *seconds*:

Dad – Annoying.

Mum – All right, but a bit stressed all the time.

Robbie – Annoying.

Susie – Annoying.

Jacob – Annoying and wet the bed again last night.

Lucy – Less annoying than the others, but she's only two so it's bound to happen.

But Mr Reeve wants us to put a bit more effort into it than that. We've got to talk about family traits and individual personalities. Blah!

After Mr Reeve and Miss Watson tell us about our assignment, we all go back to our seats. As 5W are leaving, Samir Stamford walks by my desk. He's *properly* weird. I'm not being nasty or anything. Everyone says it. He's new to our school, having moved here from Bath at the start of the term, but that's not what's weird about him. The thing is, he's

got an imaginary friend. Who he talks to. Out loud.
All the time. And the imaginary friend is called
Woody Wattler.

W-E-I-R-D, right?

'Perhaps you can ask Dad about it, while I ask
Mum?' Samir's saying to the empty space beside
him. He nods slowly. 'Not a bad idea, Woody,' he
says after a moment. 'I'll do that.'

Murphy's sat opposite me and he twirls his finger
in the air by his head, to show he thinks Samir's
properly peculiar. But Samir's not paying attention
to where he's going, and he trips over the corner of
Murphy's book bag shoved under our table. Samir
shoots his hands out to stop himself as he barges
into our table.

I jolt back a bit because Samir's hands are properly
near my arm, and I don't want him touching me.
Murphy said once that you can catch Samir's
weirdness if you touch him, and I've got enough
going on at home to worry about already.

Samir shoots us a goofy look as he props himself
back up and carries on out of the classroom. Then

he bursts out laughing, clearly at something Woody Wattler's 'said'. 'Good one,' Samir's going. 'Send 'em a postcard next time I trip up. You're a right laugh.'

Freakzoid.

Murphy starts singing a little song he's just made up:

'Samir Stamford's such a weirdo

Weirder than a purple beard-o

He thinks it's sick to be so odd

Really he's just a little—'

'Conor Murphy!' Mr Reeve booms across the classroom. 'Working hard, I see?'

Murphy picks up a pencil and leans over the table and presses his nose right up to his exercise book. 'Yes, Mr Reeve,' he says. Then he looks up at me and winks. I stifle a laugh. He's *properly* funny, is Murphy.

It's not as hard as you'd think not to talk for a day – you've just got to get used to shrugging a lot and looking down at the floor when Mr Reeve says,

'Give me five things we learned about life in the trenches yesterday. Anyone?'

There were two tricky bits, though. The first was at lunch time, when me and Murphy were sat at the table with Michael Hadley from our class and Lee Foreman from 5W. We were playing Formula One with our Capri Suns, 'cos the cartons look a bit like motor cars before you drink them, and I was Lewis Hamilton, when Murphy got his banana, shoved a bit up his nose, held his other nostril and blew the banana out all over Frankie Mellor who was sitting all alone at the end of our table. She's another purple beard-o, is Frankie. Her sister Jessica is in my class, but Frankie's in Year 6 and everyone knows who she is because she's the girl with the stammer. Like, if she's trying to say her name, she'll spend about five minutes going, 'Frr-Frrr-F-F-Frr-Fran-Fran-Fran-Frankie,' like that.

But I guess having a stammer still means you can shout OK, 'cos Frankie screamed blue flaming murder while Murphy went, 'Bogey banana all over your face!' over and over again. I almost couldn't breathe, I was doing some silent laughing – you know, when you shake your shoulders but nothing comes out of your mouth – 'cos that doesn't count as talking.

Then Mr Reeve came along, because he was on lunch duty, and said, 'I hope that's not a family trait, Mr Murphy,' and he made me and Murphy sit in separate classrooms for the rest of lunch time. And before I could even begin to *think* of protesting, Mr Reeve said, 'I don't want to hear it.' So I got away with not talking there, and I read a comic on my own and I quite enjoyed the peace and quiet, actually.

The second sticky bit came at afternoon registration. Everyone was sat on the carpet and Mr Reeve does this thing where, instead of just calling your name and you say, 'Here,' he says, 'Good afternoon, Roxy,' and Roxy will have to say, 'Good afternoon, Mr Reeve.' So I was a bit worried what I was going to do when it came to Mr Reeve saying, 'Good afternoon, Anthony,' 'cos I couldn't get away with *not* saying anything. But instead, Mr Reeve took one look at me and said, 'I know *you're* here, Anthony,' like that. So I didn't have to say anything after all. And it's funny how happy that made me.

The rest of the afternoon passed by with an ICT lesson where we had to type up instructions on the computer on 'How to Boil an Egg'. You know:

**Step 1:**    Get a saucepan.

**Step 2:**    Get an egg.

**Step 3:**    Get your mum to boil it for you.
               Ha ha ha.

But Mr Reeve told me I had to do it properly, and stop mucking about.

And then, before I knew it, it was home time. And it's a Friday, which means:

1. No more school for two whole days.

2. Fish and chips for tea.

Mint!

Mum's in the playground with Lucy fast asleep

in the buggy as I walk out of our classroom. She gives me a big smile. 'All right, love? How was school?'

I smile back at her, and she properly beams at me then, because clearly she's taken my smile to mean, 'It was brilliant, thanks for asking. I won two gold stars for being helpful and being good at listening and I ate the apple you packed me for lunch.'

She doesn't need to know the truth.

Just then, I hear someone jogging behind me. 'Mrs Button?' Mr Reeve goes, coming right up to us. 'May I have a word?'

Sheesh kebab! Mum looks at me for a moment, then says, 'Wait in the car, Anthony,' and follows Mr Reeve to the classroom.

I look on, trying to work out what all that's about. And then it dawns on me. The banana. The stupid banana.

I trudge to our purple people carrier, and open the back door. Jacob's already in there, his atlas on his lap, looking up Norway. 'All right?' he asks as I slide into my seat. He looks at me for a few seconds, clearly expecting an answer, but I don't say anything.

A few minutes later, Mum opens the back door and places Lucy in her car seat. She folds up the buggy and puts it in the boot, then slides into the driver's seat. All without saying a word. Perhaps this not-talking malarkey's catching.

Mum puts the radio on and the rest of the journey passes by with just the sound of *Absolute 80s*. A few times, I catch Mum looking at me in the rear-view mirror, and opening and closing her mouth in either an attempt to ask me something and then thinking better of it, or an attempt to do an impression of a goldfish.

As we pull into the drive, Mum switches off the engine and says, 'Jacob, can you go and tell Dad we're home?'

Jacob looks a bit confused. Perhaps Mensa need to re-examine their entry requirements. 'But he'll see the car,' he replies matter-of-factly. 'And he'll hear us when we walk in the door.'

'Can you just do it please, love?'

'And you normally shout, "We're home," when we get in,' Jacob ploughs on.

'I know, but I'm asking you to do that today. As a special favour.'

Jacob sighs and climbs out the car. Mum waits till he's shut the door and then swivels round in her seat to face me. She takes a moment, and then says, 'Anthony, is there anything you want to tell me about today?' She studies my face for a bit, but I'm not giving anything away.

And then, before she can say anything else, it all starts kicking off. Lucy wakes up and she's in that still-sleepy stage where she doesn't quite know what's going on. She can't find her dummy and starts whining. Mum tries to soothe her, but the whining turns into high-pitched screams, so I shove my hands over my ears and clamber out of the car.

'Anthony!' Mum calls after me, but I head inside and kick my shoes off.

I walk into the living room, and switch the telly on to CBBC. Brilliantly, it's *School of Silence*, a game show where kids who are properly noisy have to try and keep quiet, despite there being people popping balloons in their face and throwing custard pies at their heads. They're all pretty amateur, truth be told. I could show them a thing or two.

Badger's lying on the sofa and I flop down next to him and smooth his head as Mum comes into the front room, carrying a screaming Lucy. 'Anthony!' she says again, but Lucy's being properly loud, like *School of Silence* loud, and just then Robbie comes in from the garage, his guitar strapped to his back.

'Why aren't you still at school?' Mum asks.

Robbie shrugs. 'It's a free period.'

Mum shifts Lucy from one hip to the other, then starts searching round the front room for the dummy. 'All right, there, there,' she soothes. She looks over at Robbie. 'That's not the point. You're there to study. You've got GCSEs.'

'Stop going on,' Robbie huffs, and grabs a book of guitar music from the bookshelf in the corner. 'Everyone does it.'

'I don't,' Mum replies. '*I'm* studying for exams *and* looking after a family *and* running a household.'

Robbie just rolls his eyes while Lucy's whines get louder. Just then, Dad pops his head round the door. 'Any chance of a brew?' he asks, holding out his mug with SWINDON TOWN written on it.

'For goodness' sake!' Mum cries. 'This isn't the 1950s! Make your own tea!' But Dad just stands there looking a bit hopeless, so Mum strides into the kitchen where she shoves a carrot at Lucy to shut her up and shoves the kettle on for Dad to shut *him* up.

I'm already nicely shut up, thank you very much, and I turn back to the telly in peace and quiet.

Fish-and-chip Friday is the best. It does exactly what it says on the tin, though sometimes we're allowed to add mushy peas, or swap the fish for a saveloy if we feel like it, and Badger never bothers us for scraps 'cos he's probably the only cat in the world who doesn't like fish, which is doubly ridiculous for him as fish has bones in that he could totally choke and die on. I was a bit put off, though, because all through dinner I could feel Mum shooting looks at me every now and then. I still didn't speak, but nobody noticed.

That night, a funny thing happened. Jacob wet the bed again. Not that that's funny, mind.

I'm sleeping soundly, dreaming of playing on the wing next to Ronaldo, when I'm jolted awake by a hand shaking my shoulder.

'Anthony?' Jacob whispers, hovering by the side of my bed.

I smell the wee even before he says anything. I let out a puff of air, then get up and fling open the window.

'I don't – don't want to tell Mum,' Jacob moans. 'You won't, will you?'

I'm just about to say, "I'm pretty sure she'll find out in the morning," ' when Jacob adds, 'Seeing as you're not talking.'

Holy. Moly.

I shake my head, a bit dazed, truth be told, then get back into bed and try to get back to sleep while Jacob changes his pyjamas, grabs a pillow and lies down on the floor next to his bed so he won't get wet again.

So, Jacob's noticed my not-talking. Sheesh! But Jacob doesn't really count – it's Mum and Dad who have to.

Hmph. This may take a bit longer than I thought.

# Saturday 28 June

Today I am a Red Leicester. It's my favourite cheese. Because today I am in a MOST EXCELLENT MOOD!!!!

The reason I am a thick slab of Red Leicester tied up with a bow and a cherry on top is 'cos Mum tried to have a word with me about not talking!!!

This means my family have noticed my little protest. Sheesh kebab! I am going to have four cheese strings to celebrate.

Jacob's downstairs watching telly, and I'm lying in bed thinking about whether a hippo could kill a rhino when there's a gentle knock on the door.

Mum pops her head round. 'Can I come in?' I don't know why she bothers asking, because she's already through the door and sitting herself down on the edge of my bed before I can even say anything.

And then quickly I remember I'm not talking. Luckily.

Mum smooths down my duvet. It's red and white with the Swindon Town FC logo on it. I'm not mad keen on it, but Dad's always pleased when Mum puts it on for me. She clears her throat. 'So, Mr Reeve's word with me yesterday . . .' she says.

All of a sudden, a vision of Murphy with banana shooting out his nostril all over Frankie Mellor floats before me.

'Are you doing a sponsored silence or something I don't know about?' Mum says.

This time I'm so shocked I actually *forget* to speak.

Mum sees my confusion and ploughs on. 'Mr Reeve said you didn't say anything the whole day at school. Not during lessons, not during registration.' She frowns and her eyes are like lasers looking right through me. 'Not during the incident at lunch with Murphy and the banana.'

Blah!

I gulp, but I don't say anything. I kind of wanna see where this is going.

'And then *I* noticed you didn't say a word all evening,' Mum continues. 'Not one word.'

A few moments of silence pass between us. Mum studies my face for a long while. I shrug my shoulders and stare out the window. 'You know you can talk to me about anything, right?' Mum says.

Downstairs in the hall, the phone rings. Susie's voice shrieks out, loud and clear, 'I'LL GET IT!' Honestly, she belts it out like she's on stage at the Salisbury Playhouse. 'I SAID, I'LL GET IT. ROBBIE, GET OFF! MUM, TELL HIM! MUM!'

That's the thing about my family. Just when you think you've got your mum's undivided attention, someone else comes along – someone HIGHLY ANNOYING – and starts screeching their lungs out.

Mum lets out a sigh. She reaches out and pats my knee. 'We'll talk about this later,' she says, and she gets up off the bed.

Not if I have *my* way.

'Cos I reckon this is my thing. This is *MY THING!* Everyone's gotta have a thing, right? Like Murphy being funny. And Susie with her flaming dramatics. I could be the Boy Who Doesn't Speak. Maybe I could join a circus. Like:

# ROLL UP! ROLL UP!
## See the wonder the
## whole world
## is talking about.
## It's . . .
## The Boy Who Doesn't Speak!
## ANTHONY BUTTON
## Also in today's show, THE
## BEARDED LADY! A FIRE-
## BREATHING ELEPHANT! AND A
## MAN WITH THE WORLD'S SECOND
## LARGEST TONSILS!

# But who wants to see that when you can see
# THE BOY WHO DOESN'T SPEAK!
## DO NOT Feed the Animals.
(But the Boy Who Doesn't Speak does like cheese.)

I'll make a list of all the things I could do. There's this old man in India who's kept one arm up in the air for about twenty years, and lots of people go to see him, so I reckon I'm on to a winner, you know.

I kept up not talking all day because it's clearly working. Even Susie said, 'Why isn't Anthony saying anything?' when we all sat down for tea, and I didn't move a muscle. Ha ha! Then, a bit later, Robbie tried to annoy me and get me to shout by grabbing my hand and using it to hit my face, saying, 'Why are you hitting yourself? Why are you hitting yourself? Why are you hitting yourself?' over and over again during *Doctor Who*. I ALMOST shouted at him, but then a really good bit came on where the Doctor had to save an Ood, so EVERYONE shut up and watched it. And then Lucy gave me three of her Starbursts and a half-eaten liquorice straw 'cos she thought I was poorly. Result!

I'm going to see how long I can keep doing this. Now I know that THIS IS MY THING!

# Sunday 29 June

Today I am feeling like a bit of Wensleydale. Well, at least I
would if someone hadn't nicked it all.

It was Dad's turn to come into my room and talk to
me this morning. It went something like this:

I'm standing in front of the mirror trying to sellotape
my tongue to the back of my teeth so that I definitely
*can't* speak, especially if Robbie's going to do stupid
things like hit me in the face.

'Knock knock,' Dad says softly, and I quickly leap
from the mirror back into bed. Dad enters the room
and whips out a Superman comic from his back
pocket. 'Incidentally, I thought maybe we could

read this one together.' And he sits down on the edge of my bed. He holds the comic out to me, with this goofy, expectant grin on his face.

I mean, what can I do? There Dad is, looking all hopeful that he's going to be the one to break me. And I have to say, it's working. 'Cos I don't want to be *mean* or anything, or hurt Dad's feelings. This not talking's clearly working if Dad's buying me a comic and bothering to spend ten minutes with me reading it, like he's not done in aaaaages. The sellotape feels all tingly against my teeth anyway.

'I know it's been a crazy couple of weeks,' Dad says quietly. 'What with Ben and everything. It's been a lot to take in, for all of us. I appreciate that.' He smiles at me earnestly, and holds out the comic to me.

Too right, I think. Still. I take the comic and flick through it. Number 212, the one where Superman has this mega battle in the world of the Vanished.

Just as I'm thinking, All right, come on then,

let's get talking, Dad's mobile rings.

Dad shifts on the bed to take his mobile from his pocket and his eyes light up when he sees who's calling him. 'Ben!' he booms down the phone. 'How are you, mate?'

And before I can even say anything, before I can even go, 'All right, Dad, you've won. Here I am, talking again,' Dad's rabbiting on to Ben about us all meeting in the park that afternoon.

So I throw the comic on the bed, cross my arms and hold my tongue. Not actually, 'cos that would hurt after a while. I mean, I take out the sellotape and saliva dribbles down my chin, but I vow there and then to carry on not talking.

But Dad doesn't even notice, he's that wrapped up in his phone call.

In Ben's honour, Mum's organized a picnic in the park. ON A SUNDAY. Which means it'll be ONE WHOLE WEEK before we can have a Sunday roast again. Hmph.

AND –

Ben tucks into the picnic like he's not eaten in seven years. Honestly, I know Dad calls meal times in our family 'Feeding Time at the Zoo', but Ben's quaffed everything like he owns the place. And he didn't even bring anything. Well, one measly platter of sandwiches. And beers for Dad. And a Viennetta. Nothing interesting, anyway.

AND – this is the worst part. This is the kicker:

HE ATE THE LAST BIT OF WENSLEYDALE.

He. Ate. The. Last. Bit. Of. Wensleydale!!!!!

Everyone knows how much I love cheese. And he didn't even care! How dare he! How *dairy*! So I sit there, arms folded, and I glower at Ben for what feels like seventeen hours until finally he notices.

'What's up with Anthony?' he whispers to Dad, but I can hear what he's saying 'cos he's got such a big, fat stupid mouth.

Dad looks over to me and raises his eyebrows in mock surprise. 'Where do I start?' he says.

Well, thanks very much.

Dad laughs at my constant frowning. 'Oh, he's cheesed off about something, no doubt.'

Yes, Dad, I am cheesed off. I'm cheesed right off about the Wensleydale!

'The Incredible Sulk strikes again.' Robbie laughs and everyone joins in. I'd never really noticed before, but having two parents and four brothers and sisters and a man who doesn't belong there, all laughing at you, is a bit like a pack of wild hyenas all laughing at the zebra they're just about to eat.

## TOP 3 BUTTON FAMILY NICKNAMES, AND ONE I'VE JUST THOUGHT OF:

1. The Incredible Sulk – for me, 'cos everyone says I'm always moaning about something.
2. Einstein – for Jacob, 'cos he's so flaming brainy at everything.
3. Hooter – for Dad. You know, 'cos of his nose.
4. The Mute Button – for me. You know, 'cos I'm not talking and everything. It's pretty genius, actually, even if I do say so myself.

But then everyone stops paying attention to me because Susie and Robbie are squabbling over the last of the cocktail sausages.

'You've had loads already,' Susie says, picking up the pack of sausages and getting to her feet. She stands right on tiptoe, holding them aloft, but Robbie tackles her round the waist and they both fall back onto the picnic rug in a heap.

Mum's stressed out 'cos she forgot to bring the wet wipes and Lucy's got mucky hands. 'Pack it in, you two,' she says half-heartedly, digging in her handbag for tissues.

Robbie tickles Susie until she lets go of the sausages and he grabs them triumphantly. 'Ha!' he yells, and then he shovels a handful of them into his mouth. 'Cannhavemnoww,' he says, and he opens his mouth wide and sticks out his tongue and we all see the mashed-up sausages inside.

'My God, you're a warthog!' Susie yells.

Robbie just grins, baring all his teeth with more sausage stuck in the gaps. He swallows his mouthful, then holds the pack of sausages out to her. 'Sorry, Suze,' he says apologetically. 'I'm being mean. Here, have one.'

Susie hesitates for a moment, but then tentatively reaches forward.

Just as her fingers are finding a sausage, Robbie snatches it away from her, sticks his tongue in the pack and starts licking each and every one.

'Eeeeewwwwww, gross!' Susie squeals, and she leans forward and thumps him on the arm.

'Still want one?' Robbie asks, like butter wouldn't melt.

Ben and Dad are no help whatsoever, 'cos they just sit there, laughing. Ben has this serene kind of look on his face, like being surrounded by our crazy family is the happiest he's ever been.

Jacob's sitting under the tree over to one side of us, doing some maths puzzle or other. He's well out of it, if you ask me. Except no one *is* asking me.

'Right! Who fancies a kick-about?' Ben grins, and he reaches into his rucksack, producing a shiny new football.

Quick as a flash, Robbie shoves his trainers on, as if Roy Hodgson's on the phone calling him up for

England. Dad leaps to his feet, and even Jacob puts down his puzzle book and wanders over to us. 'May I go in goal?' he asks.

Ben ruffles his hair. 'Course you can, champ.' Then he looks at me. 'You joining in?'

I shake my head.

Lucy climbs onto Mum's lap. 'Go on, love,' Mum says to me.

I had a properly genius idea this morning, when I knew we'd be coming here. I went over to my wardrobe and dug out the notepad that Auntie Shelley got me last Christmas. It's got a picture of Transformers on the front, but you can't have everything. I take the pad out of the back pocket of my jeans and scribble something on it. Then I hold it up for everyone to see.

'Can't-be-bothered,' Susie reads, squinting to decipher my handwriting.

'You sure, mate?' Ben asks. He looks at me like he's disappointed, but I reckon he's just putting that on. Like I reckon he ate the last bit of Wensleydale just to be mean.

'Oh, leave him,' Susie sighs, grabbing a hairband from round her wrist and scraping her hair back into a ponytail. 'He's just attention-seeking.'

Which is rich, coming from her.

Dad gives me this little smile, then he and Ben and Jacob and Susie and Robbie head off to play their stupid game of football. 'Boys against girls?' Ben says.

'Hey! That's not fair!' Susie laughs, pushing him playfully.

I actually think I feel sick. And not just from the stupid Viennetta. I turn to Mum to beam at her that it's just me and her now and maybe we can have some quality time together, but her eyes are closed and her head's drooping on top of Lucy's.

So I'm left all on my own, again.

This is when I get my brilliant plan.

It's called OPERATION GROB.

Get. Rid. Of. Ben.

Things were so much better before Ben and his brilliant football skills turned up.

OPERATION GROB: Get. Rid. Of. Ben.

- Hire an assassin.
- Pretend we've moved.
- Make him allergic to us so he can't bear to be around us.
- Wait until Badger eventually tops himself and blame it on Ben.
- Do another DNA test, like they're always doing on *Jeremy Kyle*, and fake the results. 'Sorry, Ben, you're not Dad's son after all. Now push off.'

It's a work in progress, admittedly. About eighty-nine hours later, everyone traipses back from playing football. Jacob's on Dad's shoulders, like he's just scored the winning goal against Reading in the Championship. Ben's giving Susie a piggyback and zigzagging his way over to us, which is ridiculous 'cos he's treating her like she's four. Maybe he's so stupid he's got her and Lucy mixed up. Robbie comes bounding over, and the noise wakes Mum with a start.

'Whattimeisit?' she asks, all sleepy.

'HOLIDAY TIME!' Robbie yells.

Mum wipes sleep from her eyes. 'You told them, then?' she says to Dad.

I almost forget myself, 'cos I'm so curious and I almost – ALMOST – say, 'Told them what?'

Everyone plonks themselves down on the picnic rug. Robbie rummages in the cool box and grazes on the leftover bits of quiche. 'A-aa-a-choooo!' He lets rip a ferocious sneeze.

Operation GROB in action! I'd put pepper in the quiche to activate my 'Make Ben Allergic to Us' plan. Oops. Still, serves Robbie right for his 'Incredible Sulk' comment.

'Dad said we can have a holiday this year.' Susie beams at me. 'I'm thinking Hollywood.'

'Steady on,' Mum says, and she frowns at Dad. 'I'm thinking more of a Staycation. A nice camping trip to Cornwall or something.'

Robbie rolls his eyes. Which is quite hard for him to do, 'cos they're streaming with tears. 'Or something,' he sniffs.

Susie sticks out her bottom lip. 'Oh, pleeeeeeeee-eeeeeeeeease. I could get spotted! Steven Spielberg might see me in a restaurant and cast me in his next film. Then we'd be rich!'

Mum looks over to me. 'What do you think, Anthony? Fancy a holiday this year?'

I nod, 'cos any time away from Ben sounds ACE to me.

'Where would you like to go? You fancy camping?'

Before I can nod my head, Susie leaps to her feet like she's sat on a bee. Which I know all about, because I did that two years ago when a bee landed on the saddle of my bike and I didn't see it, and I sat on it and it stung me, right on the bum. But I'd sat down so hard that I'd squashed it and it died, so justice was done in the end.

'Don't answer that, Anthony!' Susie screams at me, and she grabs my elbow and hoists me to my feet. 'Everyone, with me!'

She marches me off to the corner of the park, and I look behind to see Jacob and Robbie traipsing after us.

'We're going to get Anthony the best deal,' she bleats, making us form a huddle. 'I'll be your agent.'

'What are you talking about?' Robbie says, pushing his fringe out of his eyes. They're still all red and watery.

'It's clear that this is a parental ploy,' Susie replies. 'Yes, it's great that Mum and Dad say we can have a holiday, but can't you see, this is really just a way of getting Anthony to talk?'

'It is?' Robbie frowns. 'And Anthony's not talking?'

Well, thanks for noticing, stupid.

Then he flashes me a grin, making it clear he knew all along, and I feel a teensy bit guilty about the whole pepper-in-the-quiche thing.

'I agree,' Jacob says, nodding wisely. 'It's a bargaining tool, certainly.'

'So let's see how far we can get Mum and Dad to go.' Susie beams. Then she cranes her neck and calls out, 'BEN! You should be here for this.'

Just when I was starting to like her.

Ben comes running over, and bursts into our huddle like he's got every right to be there. 'What's going on?'

'We're holding out for a better holiday,' Robbie says. 'Anthony's not to talk until Mum and Dad say we can go somewhere better than camping in Cornwall.'

I scribble something on my pad then, and just as I'm about to hold it up to show everyone, Ben blurts out, 'But I *like* camping in Cornwall.'

So I shove my pad back in my pocket without showing anyone.

'What about Disneyland?' Susie says. 'I'm sure there'll be film producers there.'

Robbie rubs his chin. 'Yeah, I could do that. Agreed?'

He looks around the circle. Jacob opens his mouth to say something, then thinks better of it. 'Agreed,' he says softly, looking down at the floor.

'Ben? You won't tell Mum and Dad?' Susie asks. 'Swear?'

Ben solemnly crosses his heart.

Robbie holds out his hand, palm down. Susie slaps hers on top of it. Then Jacob, then Ben. 'So then, Anthony,' Robbie says. 'You don't talk until we can get Mum and Dad to agree to take us to Disneyland. Think you can do that?'

My stomach flips over because I'm so excited. No, more than that. I'm – *proud*. I'm so pleased that everyone's asking *me* to do something. *I'm* the one who can make or break the Button Family Holiday this year. The Buttons are counting on *me*! I beam at them and slap my hand on top of Ben's. Extra-hard, 'cos it's his hand.

'Gooooooooooooooooooo, TEAM!' Susie yells, and we push our hands up into the air.

'Kids! Time to go!' Mum calls, and she starts packing up the picnic bits.

Two minutes later, Susie's practically skipping alongside Ben, the picnic blanket rolled under her arm; Jacob and Robbie are chatting animatedly about planes as they balance the Tupperware boxes, and I trail after them. I flip open my notepad to the page I just wrote on and read back over it:

## BUT I *LIKE* CAMPING IN CORNWALL

I tear the page out of the notepad and screw it up into a ball, just as Mum thrusts the cool box at me. So I shove the pad in my back pocket and the screwed-up piece of paper into the cool box, like a bin, and bung it in the boot. 'Cos I don't want ANYONE to know that I wrote the Exact Same Thing that Ben said. I don't know what I was thinking.

But I can't worry too much about stupid old Ben, because I've got some serious not-talking to do. Not only is Not Talking now MY THING, but Robbie and Susie and Jacob are relying on me. Me! I'm going to get us all a decent holiday! I'm going to be the BIG CHEESE in this family!

It's about flaming time.

# Monday 30 June

Today I am the Manchego DO Gran Reserva.
Quite simply 'cos it's officially the best cheese in the world.

So I've got to keep on not talking until I can get us a holiday to Disneyland. That's a step up from three squashed Starbursts and a half-eaten liquorice straw.

In the kitchen, Robbie and Susie are being super-weird. They're sat round the table eating breakfast and everything. Normally, if you've got a spare two minutes between queuing for the bathroom and trying to find your textbooks, you might shove a Weetabix in your mouth.

But Robbie's holding out a plate of toast to Susie

and going, 'Would you like another slice?' And she politely declines and goes, 'Let me pass you the sugar,' and Robbie takes a spoonful and stirs it in his coffee.

Mum and Dad exchange a look. 'Well, this is nice, isn't it?' Dad says. 'Anthony, what would you like to eat?'

Susie leaps up at that and scrapes back a chair. 'Usual, Anthony?'

I nod, a bit dazed, truth be told, and sit down while Susie fixes me a bowl of Rice Krispies.

'Only the best for my favourite brother,' Robbie says with a grin.

Dad's eyebrows shoot upwards like they've got a mind of their own. Susie throws Robbie a look as she plonks the bowl of cereal in front of me, then traces her finger along her neck as if to say, 'SHUT UP!' She clearly thinks he's overdoing it.

Mum rubs her hand over her forehead. 'All right, Ant. This has gone on long enough.'

Dad shakes his head at her. 'Clare. Come on.'

'I mean it,' Mum says to me. 'Just say something.'

I look at Mum and Dad and then at Robbie and Susie.

Robbie silently mouths, 'DIS–NEY–LAND.'

'What if we said we'd buy you a new game for the Xbox?' Dad pipes up. 'Anything you want. Your choice. Hmm? Why don't you tell us what you want?'

They both hold their breath and wait for me to speak. From the corner of my eye, I see Susie bite her lip.

I shrug my shoulders.

Mum lets out a puff of air and gets up from the table. 'I've just got to check on Lucy,' she announces, strangely formally, and moves to the door. 'Phil!'

Dad doesn't do anything for a moment, just drains the coffee from his cup.

'Phil!' Mum barks again.

He looks up at her, and it slowly clicks. 'Right,' he says, scraping back his chair. 'I'll – give you a hand.' And he leaves the kitchen too.

Robbie leans in to me and Susie. 'They're so obvious.'

'*You're* so obvious,' Susie hisses. 'You're being far too nice. They know something's up.'

We all sit there in silence, which is exactly the position I started off in, so no change there. Mum and Dad speak in low murmurs in the hall, but we can still hear them. I guess we don't really do 'subtle' in our family. Maybe I'll make a note of that for the presentation.

'. . . thought he was just having a bit of a sulk at first . . . going on for days now,' Mum whispers. '. . . don't know what more we can do.'

Robbie gives me and Susie the thumbs up across the table. 'Disneyland, here we come,' he grins.

I beam back at him. This'll keep me in everyone's good books for at least the next twelve years. Guess I'm not so stupid now, am I?

'. . . what if it's medical?' Mum whispers out in the hall. 'What if it's psychological?'

Dad sighs. '. . . he'll come round, love. Come on . . . oh no, don't do that . . .'

And then there's a bit of rustling, and some-one gives a loud sniff and blows their nose loudly.

I think it's Dad. He *has* got a bit of a hooter on him.

As Robbie sits there finishing his coffee, I catch Susie's eye. She's frowning, ever so slightly.

I know how she feels. As much as I'm enjoying all this special attention, and Robbie and Susie being nice to me like never, I don't want Dad to *cry* over it or anything.

Before I can write anything down on my notepad, Dad leans round the kitchen door and his eyes don't look at all teary, so he can't be that fussed after all. 'Right, you lot,' he booms. 'School.'

And I have to traipse off to get ready for another boring week at Furton Yarrow Primary.

The main item on today's agenda was this flaming 'My Family and Other Animals' presentation they're making Year 5 do. Mr Reeve says it's not enough to talk about your immediate family members but that we should try and do a bit of research into our family tree, and find out about our ancestors, with special emphasis on if any of them fought in the

First World War, seeing as that's our topic for the term. And then we have to talk for three minutes about our findings.

But here's the worst part. Here's the kicker —

WE HAVE TO DO IT IN FRONT OF OUR FAMILIES!!!!!

It's a proper presentation, to be held in the school hall on the evening of 10 July. Which is only TEN DAYS away.

HOLY MOLY!

It's all anyone can talk about. Well, not me, obviously. At lunch, everyone's gone a bit family-tree mad, going around saying, 'Who do you think you are?' and 'Don't you know who I am?' like it's the funniest thing on earth. And, 'I bet you a fiver I'm related to Kate Middleton.' That was Jemima — she's well posh. She's got a swimming pool in her back garden, so she might well be, you know.

We're sitting in the canteen, and I'm halfway through my Lincolnshire Poacher cheese sandwich, when Murphy leans over the table. He has hot dinners every day, and he always manages to get most of it down him. He's worse than Lucy.

'Why aren't you talking, Ant?' Murphy says, flicking at a kernel of sweetcorn stuck to his tie. Murphy is someone Mum describes as 'not one to mince his words'. She says that's the Irish in him, and how I've got to be careful 'cos he's got the gift of the gab and can talk his way out of anything, whereas I'm not talking at all. Michael Hadley and Lee Foreman lean in too, obviously waiting on some juicy gossip.

I shrug my shoulders, and carry on munching my sandwich. 'Why are you being all weird, then?' Murphy says.

I let out a sigh and reach into the pocket of my trousers. I quickly scribble on my Transformers notepad:

IT'S JUST AN EXPERIMENT I'M CONDUCTING
ON MY FAMILY

And hold it up for them to see.

They take a few moments to read it, and then look at each other blankly.

'Well, why didn't you say so?' Michael laughs, and the three of them go back to eating their lunch.

There's a small bead of sweat trickling down my back, and it takes me a minute to work out that I was nervous, actually *nervous* of what they'd think of me. Strange. But now I know they don't really think I'm weirder than a purple beard-o, I feel a whole lot better.

AND I reckon if I keep up this no talking malarkey, I won't have to do this stupid 'My Family and Other Animals' presentation, either. What's Mr Reeve going to do? Stand me in front of all the mums and dads and move my jaw around for me? He can't *make* me talk!

So all I've got to do is NOT TALK, and then I can:

1. Get to Disneyland.
   And
2. Get out of this flaming presentation.

Suddenly I feel a whole lot better about everything.

Then Mrs Wintour, the teaching assistant, comes over to our table. 'Anthony, dear,' she says, 'pick up your bag and head to reception. Your mum's taking you out of school for the afternoon.'

Sheesh. Kebab!

Murphy, Michael and Lee look at me, their eyes wide. 'Is this for the experiment?' Michael whispers.

I shrug my shoulders again and wave goodbye to them, hoping that I'm really not going to be tested on like a lab rat.

Mum's sitting in a chair in reception, the buggy parked next to her. 'All right, love?' she says as I traipse over. 'Got everything?'

I nod and reach into my trouser pocket. I quickly scribble on my notepad:

### WHERE ARE WE GOING?

Mum reads it and yawns.

Well, thanks very much.

'Oh, sorry,' she says, covering her mouth with her hand. 'I'm shattered.' She smiles. 'You'll see.'

And she leads me out of reception to the car park.

I'm sitting in Dr Price's room at the medical practice down the road from our house. Dr Price has been our family doctor since I was born, and even before then. He's dead old. Like fifty. He looks like he should be *taking* medication, not prescribing it.

'And why do you think that is, young Anthony?' Dr Price says, peering over his desk and looking right at me. He presses his spindly fingers together, like he's about to start praying.

I might start praying 'cos Dr Price is doing what he always does: treating me like a baby. Maybe he's so old he's got me mixed up with Jacob and thinks I still wet the bed too.

I shrug my shoulders. Mum, sitting on the chair next to me, with Lucy crawling over her lap, takes a sharp breath.

Dr Price taps his fingers against his chin, as if he's

thinking deeply. 'There must be a reason why you don't want to talk,' he presses.

I shrug my shoulders again. 'Oh, for goodness' sake,' Mum mutters under her breath, but I catch her.

'Anthony?' Dr Price repeats.

I shrug once more. This time, Mum's not so quiet. 'Please, Anthony,' she hisses. 'I'm too tired for this.'

Dr Price turns his attention to Mum and smiles kindly. 'It's OK, Mrs Button. I understand you're concerned—'

'Exasperated, more like,' Mum sighs quietly.

There's that word again. *Exasperated*. People seem to use that a lot around me.

'Anthony,' Dr Price says, but he doesn't take his eyes off Mum, 'why don't you step outside, like a good boy, while I have a word with your mummy.'

*Mummy?* Puh-lease!

I leap to my feet, glad to escape, pick up my school bag and trudge outside.

It's not till the next day that I find out exactly what this word Dr Price had with 'Mummy' was.

# Tuesday 1 July

Today I am a Jarlsberg cheese. It's a bit nutty.
And today has been more than a bit nutty.
Things I learned: 'Wits' end' is not a place like Land's End,
even though it's somewhere your mum can be at.

I got taken out of school again. This time, EVERYONE noticed, not just Murphy and Michael and Lee.

It's 11.42 and the rest of the class are working on their Family Tree, but I'm just flicking through a comic.

Stacy catches what I'm doing and she whispers, 'Why aren't you working on your presentation, Ant? Have you done it already?'

I shake my head and scribble on my Transformers notepad:

I'LL STILL BE DOING EXPERIMENT THEN. WON'T BE TALKING. WON'T HAVE TO DO STUPID PRESENTATION.

Stacy exchanges a look with Michael, but before anyone can say anything, Mrs Wintour comes over to our table and leans in to whisper to me.

'Anthony, love,' she says, and I can tell Michael and Stacy and Murphy are pretending they're not listening, 'it's time for you to head to reception.'

I look at her in shock. 'You know,' she prompts. 'For your appointment.'

I'm too astonished to blurt out, 'WHAT APPOINTMENT???' but it wouldn't matter anyway, 'cos Mrs Wintour's already off to Neptune table to tell Amy Mason to give Lauren Allen back her fluffy pen.

When she's out of earshot, Michael looks at me slyly. 'You're dead lucky, you know,' he says. 'Being taken out of school all the time.'

Stacy looks over to him. 'Shhhhh,' she hisses. 'Mr Reeve said we're not to talk about it.'

Well, that totally throws me.

TALK ABOUT WHAT?

Stacy looks over to Neptune table to check that both Mr Reeve and Mrs Wintour can't hear. 'We're not s'posed to go on about it,' she whispers conspiratorially, 'but when you were out yesterday afternoon, Mr Reeve told us not to worry about you not talking, and to just let you get on with it, and not to make a big deal about it and mostly to leave you alone for it.'

Wow. Michael and Stacy can tell by my face that this is obviously news to me.

This whole time, Murphy's not said a word, and for a moment I wonder if he's copying me with the not talking. He's just been staring at his worksheet and scowling.

But as I'm shaking my head in disbelief at the fact that Mr Reeve's had a word with the whole class about me, Murphy looks up. 'We're meant to be playing footie at lunch,' he mutters.

'Anthony!' Mrs Wintour calls from the other side of the room. 'Time to go!' Well, considering 5R aren't meant to be going on about it, Mrs Wintour's made such a racket that the whole class turns to look at me.

I let out a sigh and stuff my notepad and pencil case into my bag.

Murphy carries on scowling. 'Fine,' he huffs. 'Michael can be in centre, then, if you're not gonna be here.' And he smiles pointedly. I can tell he's dead annoyed at me.

I get up from the table, pick up my bag and walk out of the classroom. 'Bye, Ant!' Stacy calls after me. I'm too upset to wave back at her.

But when I get to reception, I can't help but smile. Standing there, studying the Year 3 'Creatures of the Deep' collage on the display board, is Dad.

'All right, Anthony?' He beams as I trudge over. Dad says 'Cheerio' to Mrs Hurst in the school office and holds the front door open for me. 'I expect you're wondering what we're up to,' he says, digging his car keys out of his pocket.

I slide into the front seat of our people carrier as Dad climbs into the driver's seat.

'We're off to see a child psychologist,' he says matter-of-factly.

WHAT?????

Dad clearly sees the panic flash across my face, because he holds up his hands. 'Don't worry, don't worry,' he says quickly. 'You've not done anything wrong. It'll be a quick meeting, and they'll just want to ask you a couple of questions. Nothing to worry about, all right? And then we'll go out for a bite to eat afterwards. What do you say?'

I mull it over for a second, then take out my notepad and grab a pen from the glove box.

## CAN IT BE PIZZA?

Dad reads the note and laughs. '*That's* the only question you have about all this?' He shakes his head in amazement. 'My boy,' he booms, 'you are a marvel.'

He sticks the key in the ignition and starts the

car and we zoom along listening to some old band called Travis Dad always listens to.

The Furton Yarrow Child Psychology and Speech Therapy Practice is right on the edge of town. The building's all glass on the outside and they've got a revolving door, which Dad got stuck in 'cos he tried to nip in right behind me and didn't walk round quickly enough. I did some silent laughter at that. Especially 'cos he sort of tumbled out into the reception area.

The practice is dead quiet, and has the sort of beige marble floor where all you can hear is CLACK CLACK CLACK when someone walks across it. The receptionist smiles at us from behind her wooden desk as we walk (and tumble) in.

'Anthony Button,' Dad says to her, taking something from his trouser pocket. It's a nappy. Is there *nothing* Mum won't write on? 'We've got an appointment with' – he peers at Mum's handwriting – 'sorry about this ... er ... Dr Moriarty, is that?'

The evil guy from *Sherlock*? Blah! Where are Mum and Dad sending me???

'Morley,' the receptionist replies with a smile. 'Take a seat.' She gestures to a row of chairs along the back wall.

We CLACK CLACK CLACK our way across reception and plonk ourselves down and Dad picks up a *What Car?* magazine from the coffee table. There's a corridor leading off from the reception area, and several doors along the corridor.

'Hey, Ant,' Dad whispers. 'You'll like this. What car magazine sold one million copies last year?'

I shrug my shoulders.

Dad smiles. 'No, it's a joke. You're meant to say, "I don't know, Dad, what car magazine sold one million copies last year?"'

I shrug my shoulders again.

'No – *what car* magazine,' Dad repeats, and he waves *What Car?* magazine in my face. 'Get it? What car magazine has sold one million . . . ? Oh, never mind.' He lets out a puff of air.

I look at the clock on the wall and follow the second hand round. We've been sat there for four minutes and twenty-nine seconds when a tall girl with blonde hair walks into reception and heads for the wooden desk.

I don't take much notice of her at first, but it's so quiet I can't help but hear her.

'Frrrrr,' she goes. 'Frrrrr.'

It's Frankie Mellor. Stammering Frankie Mellor!

Frankie's mum's standing behind her and neither she nor the receptionist say anything, but wait for Frankie to finish.

'Frrrrr—' Frankie stutters again, and her face is going all red and she looks dead annoyed with herself. 'Frrrannnnk–kkkkeee,' she says eventually. And then she takes a few deep breaths and says, all in one go, 'Frrrrraaaaann-kie Melllll-or.'

Her mum beams at her as the receptionist gestures for them to take a seat.

Frankie and Mrs Mellor sit down opposite us, and when Frankie catches my eye she immediately looks down and messes with her hair so that it now covers her face and I can't really see her properly.

Just then, one of the doors off the corridor opens and out waltzes –

Samir Stamford. King of the purple beard-os, Samir Stamford. Well, isn't this just a regular Furton Yarrow Primary School reunion?

'Bye, Jess,' Samir says to whoever's inside the room he's just come out of, and he looks up at the empty space next to him. 'You're telling me, Woody Wattler,' he says and stifles a laugh. Then he spots me, and his face lights up. 'Anthony!' he booms, and he marches over. I shrink back a bit in my chair so he can't touch me. 'Fancy seeing you here!' And *then* he spots Frankie Mellor and he practically has a fit. 'Frankie!' He opens his arms wide as if he's expecting a group hug. Frankie mumbles something to herself and her face goes bright red. 'You seeing Jess?' Samir asks me. He leans in to the space beside him, and nods. 'I mean, Dr Morley,' he corrects himself.

I nod, a little dazed, truth be told.

'She's great.' Samir smiles. 'You'll love her.' And with that he skips off out of reception. CLACK CLACK CLACKETY-CLACK. 'See you at school,' he shouts back at both of us.

I look over to Frankie, but she's staring down at the ground as if there's something totally and utterly fascinating down there.

'Anthony Button?' a voice to my left says softly.

A woman stands in the doorway of the room Samir just came out of. Dad squeezes my knee and we both get up from our chairs.

Meeting Dr Morley wasn't as traumatic as you'd think. She's actually pretty cool. She had a little chat with Dad first of all. I think it was to let him know what she'd be making me do in our meeting. Then Dad waited outside on the chair, finishing his magazine, while me and Jess talked in her office. Well, she talked and I made notes every now and then.

She said I was allowed to call her Jess, because it's less formal. She's got hair like:

'cos it's dark brown and wavy. She has big blue eyes and a little mole above her top lip like this:

And she doesn't look that old. Younger than Mum anyway. And even though she's got a desk in her office, she doesn't sit behind it, she sits next to it, opposite me, 'cos she says she doesn't want to 'put a barrier between us'.

Jess explained that she's trained in listening to children talk about what's going on in their lives, and I'm allowed to ask any questions I want at any time, and if I want to go home at any time, that's fine too. And then we played a word association game. She saw that I had a notepad and pen of my own, so she said a word and I'd have to write down

the first thing that popped into my head. It went
like this:

| Jess: | Dinosaur | Me: | BONES |
| Jess: | Water | Me: | BOMB |
| Jess: | Pizza | Me: | CHEESE |
| Jess: | School | Me: | BORING |
| Jess: | Circle | Me: | CHEESE |
| Jess: | Friends | Me: | MORE |
| Jess: | Talent | Me: | NONE |
| Jess: | Brother | Me: | ANNOYING |
| Jess: | Dad | Me: | BUSY |
| Jess: | Wheel | Me: | CHEESE |
| Jess: | Sister | Me: | ANNOYING |
| Jess: | Teacher | Me: | MEAN |
| Jess: | Mum | Me: | STRESSED |
| Jess: | House | Me: | CHEESE |

I got a bit side-tracked by the last one, 'cos
my tummy rumbled. The game's just a bit of
fun, really. I was writing down any old word.
It doesn't mean anything. Except that I like

cheese, I suppose, but we knew that already.

At the end, Jess said she'd like me to come back for more sessions. I don't know why. Perhaps she likes playing the game. Then she reached into the drawer of her desk and picked out a book, passing it to me.

It's a journal. It's got a green cover and PROPERTY OF written across the front in graffiti. The pages are all blank, except for PERSONAL DETAILS on the first page.

Jess says I have to use the journal to write down my feelings, if I won't talk about them. She says I don't have to show her *everything*, but at my next session she'd like me to show her at least one thing from it, and we'll go from there.

It all seems like a boring waste of time to me.

What totally makes up for everything is going out for pizza with Dad. We don't go to Pizza Express, 'cos Mum's told Dad to have only a 'light bite' and not spoil our appetites for dinner. We go to this little café down the road from the psychology practice and they've only got mushroom pizza or ham and pineapple. No cheese! Fancy doing pizza and not having any cheese! When we waltz into the café, a little bell above the door goes 'TRIIIIIIINNNNG' like that, and the waiter comes over to seat us.

He stops before he gets to us, and his smile freezes. 'Pizza Express,' he goes, the colour draining from his face, 'the other night.' And he looks like he's having a breakdown.

'Oh yeah!' Dad laughs. 'You were our waiter. Sorry about the racket!' And he plonks himself down at a table for two.

The waiter looks at us in a daze. 'Will this be a regular occurrence, sir?'

I sit down opposite Dad as he studies my face. 'For now,' he says, and I beam back at him. The waiter drifts back to the counter and takes off his apron. He picks up his coat from the coat rack and marches out of the door.

Still, I'm grinning at Dad as he yaks on about Swindon's chances this season and all *I* can think about is: If this is what it takes for a one-to-one with Dad; if *this* is what I have to do to spend a bit of quality time with him, just me and him, like we NEVER do EVER, with no one else annoying us, or bleating on about acting or guitars or maths puzzles or *Peppa Pig* or flaming Hunter & Sons, well, I might just keep up this child psychologist malarkey, you know.

# Tuesday 1 July

## 4.30 p.m.

At home, Mum's all smiles when we get in, and she stands in the kitchen doorway holding a dessert plate. 'Cheesecake,' she says, like I'm blind and can't tell. 'Your favourite.' She looks from me to Dad. 'Was everything . . . OK?'

Dad shrugs his shoulders. 'He liked the pizza,' is all he says.

Mum bites her lip. 'Anything you want to tell us?'

When I don't answer, Mum nods slowly. 'Right. Well. I'd better make a start on tea. Where's the fish?'

Dad claps a hand to his mouth.

Mum puts the cheesecake down on the table and folds her arms. 'You forgot the fish.' It's not a question.

So after a bit of yelling, Mum hands me and Susie a tenner and makes us pootle off to Tesco. I'm tempted to write a note, saying:

## WHAT DID YOUR LAST SERVANT DIE OF?

but my hand's a bit sore from all the writing I did this afternoon.

Something funny happens at the supermarket. All the way there, Susie's going on about her school summer play. It's *Annie* and Susie's the lead, naturally. Though I think it's partly 'cos she's got red hair and it saves on buying a wig.

The man behind the fish counter at Tesco is big and burly and looks like he'd rather be anywhere else in the world than right here, among the haddock and the mussels, in a white apron and hat. 'What you after?' he asks us with a sigh.

I hold up my finger, as if to say, 'Hang on a minute, good sir,' and reach into my trouser pocket for my notepad. 'Cept it's not there. I reach into the other pocket. Not there, either. I pat my trousers down, then my school shirt, but it's nowhere to be found. I must have left it at home, or in the car.

The man behind the counter lets out a big puff of air. 'Any time today, kids,' he moans.

Susie shoots him a look. 'He's an elective mute,' she says matter-of-factly. 'It means he's choosing not to speak and this is a very difficult time for all our family, thank you very much.' She looks over to me and stifles a grin as the man opens his mouth in shock.

'I'm — I'm sorry,' he splutters. 'Do — do you want to point to what you're after?' And he gestures to all the fish behind the counter.

Susie shakes her head. 'He'd prefer to act it out,' she says, and I look at her in horror. 'Go on.' She nudges me forward.

Well. What can I say? The man behind the counter looks at both of us as if we're oddballs, and

I stand there with my mouth open in a perfect 'o'. Not because that's my impression of a fish, but 'cos I'm so surprised, truth be told.

'That could be anything,' the man behind the counter says. He's got a point.

So I put down my basket and grin at him, as big a grin as I can do, until my cheeks start to ache. The man scratches his head. 'Smile?' he asks, confused. 'There's no such fish as a smile.'

Behind me, I can hear Susie giggling away. Then, being the actress that she is, she decides to join in. 'Are you sure it's not this, Anthony?' she laughs, and she starts sliding up and down in front of the counter, like she's on an ice rink.

'Now that one I know,' the man behind the counter says and there's a little twinkle in his eye, as if he's actually starting to have fun. 'Skate!' he cries, pointing at Susie. 'Skate!'

I shake my head, and carry on grinning. Seriously, the man had better hurry up, 'cos my cheeks can't take much more of this. I can feel them getting all hot too, 'cos people are starting to stare.

Susie stops skating, and instead mimes being a saxophone player. 'Music!' the fish man shouts, and he's properly enjoying himself now. 'Saxophone!'

An old woman joins us at the counter and leans heavily on her shopping trolley. 'Song?' she guesses, a bemused look on her face. A man about Dad's age walks up to us, his daughter sitting on top of his shoulders. 'What's going on?'

A voice pipes up behind me. 'We're playing charades,' a posh woman says. 'We're guessing what fish these children want.' I look behind me then, and there's a little crowd gathered now. I can feel myself going bright red at all this attention, but Susie's loving it, miming playing the trumpet, then singing, as if with a microphone. It properly looks like she's on *The X Factor*.

'Tune!' a man in a blue shirt says. He's wearing a little badge saying: KEVIN. STORE MANAGER. HAPPY TO HELP.

The man behind the counter smacks his forehead. 'Tuna!' he cries. 'Is that it?'

I shake my head. I relax my cheeks a little, rub my jaw and start grinning again, wider this time. I point to my mouth.

'Face?' someone in the crowd guesses. 'Pain? Face ache? Hake!'

I grit my teeth and carry on smiling.

'Grin?'

'Beam!' the old woman with the trolley shouts. She claps her hands in delight. 'He's beaming!'

The man behind the counter punches his fist in the air. 'BREAM!' he yells, and I look around and EVERYONE in the supermarket is looking over at us, wondering what the heck is going on.

'Is that it?' Fish Man asks. 'Is it bream?'

I relax my cheeks and look at the crowd. They all hold their breath as one.

Then I nod and everyone bursts into applause.

'Bream!' they mutter to each other, chatting excitedly. 'Well I never!'

The man reaches inside the counter and pulls out a plate of fish with a little flag on it saying: SEA BREAM.

The crowd starts to drift away, until it's only me and Susie and the woman with the trolley left.

'There you go, son,' the man behind the counter says, bagging up the fish and handing it to me with a grin. 'Most fun I've had at work in ages.' He looks to the woman with the trolley. 'And what can I get you, my love?' He's in the most marvellous mood.

The old woman starts miming that she's a pirate with a sword. Fish Man frowns at her. 'Don't you start,' he grumbles.

I place the bag in the basket and we walk towards the check-out. 'That was ace!' Susie whispers, leaning in to me, a huge beam on her face. Or *bream*, I suppose. Just then she stops stock-still in the middle of the supermarket and her face darkens. 'Quick!' she hisses, grabbing me by the shirt sleeve. 'In here.' She yanks me into the cereal aisle and makes me duck down behind a stack of Coco Pops.

I look at her in surprise, but she keeps her eyes on the floor. Inside I'm kicking myself for forgetting my notepad, 'cos if I had it, I'd write:

## WHAT'S ALL THIS ABOUT?

Instead, I sneak a glance at what she's so keen to avoid, but all I can see are two girls, one about double the size of the other, both wearing the same school uniform as Susie. They're loitering by the confectionery aisle, and after a moment they both grab a bag of Maltesers and a bag of Haribo. What a balanced diet.

Susie's frowning at them and biting down on her nails, and as she shifts her weight, 'cos crouching is obviously hurting her as much as it's hurting me, she accidentally knocks into the stack of Coco Pops and they all topple to the ground.

Susie lets out a yelp and before we know it, the girls are standing over us.

'All right, ginge?' the big one smirks. Her eyes shine fiercely at us. Susie goes very still at that.

'What, not laughing?' the other oaf says. 'Can't take a joke?'

Susie looks down at the floor and doesn't say anything, which isn't like her. Dad says she's always got an answer for everything.

'I thought you were never fully dressed without a smile, Annie,' the first girl says, and the two of them laugh like the peculiars they are.

Susie blinks really hard and has the sort of look on her face that I would have if someone told me the world was going to run out of cheese in approximately three days.

The big girl nudges me with her foot. 'Who's this? Another one of the Button freaks?'

Well, really.

The smaller girl peers at me curiously. 'Why aren't you saying anything? Can't you talk or something?'

The big girl snorts. 'He's a freak just like her, isn't he?' She glares at Susie. 'Isn't he, Annie?'

Susie keeps her head down, but I can see her eyes are starting to brim with tears.

Well – I'm not having that. Nobody slights me and the good Button family name. No one!

'DEATH BY CEREAL!!!!' I scream at them silently inside my head and before I know it, I'm picking up a box of Coco Pops and lobbing it at the girls.

Susie claps her hand to her mouth in shock as the box flies through the air and smacks the big girl on the side of the head.

'Owwwwww!' she shouts in surprise.

So I lob another. And then another. And all the time the girls are stumbling backwards amid flying boxes of Coco Pops and I'm charging down the aisle and grabbing whatever I can get my hands on, and throwing packets of Ryvita and Quavers and All-Bran, like POW! POW! POW! And they're going SMACK! SMACK! SMACK! on the girls' heads and knees and faces. DEATH BY GO-AHEAD BARS!

It's pretty ace, truth be told. I feel like a ninja! Or James Bond. But, you know, with cereal instead of guns and exploding toothpaste. I'm going to add it to my list.

THINGS THAT COULD BE 'MY THING'
- JOIN THE CIRCUS AND BE A SIDESHOW ACT AS THE BOY WHO DOESN'T SPEAK. MIGHT NEED TO DO THIS FOR TWENTY YEARS LIKE THAT MAN IN INDIA WITH HIS ARM IN THE AIR

- SPY & ASSASSIN, LIKE JAMES BOND?
- NINJA!!! SPECIALITY — THROWING CEREAL BOXES AT PEOPLE'S HEADS. MIGHT NEED TO PRACTISE MY AIM 'COS SOME OF THE BOXES HIT THE GIRLS ON THEIR KNEES AND TOES AND ELBOWS INSTEAD. WHERE DO YOU GO TO TRAIN TO BE A NINJA? NOTE — FIND OUT HOW TO SIGN UP FOR NINJA CLASSES.

Then Kevin, with his little STORE MANAGER, HAPPY TO HELP badge comes marching over, his face like thunder, and shoos us all the way out of the store, before we can even say that we haven't paid for the fish yet.

Result! I'm keeping the tenner and Mum never needs to know!

We walk home in complete silence, and Susie keeps glancing over her shoulder every now and then.

As we're rounding the corner of Abbeville Road, not far from our street, Susie bites her bottom lip.

'About what just happened,' she says really quietly, and I struggle to hear her over the sound of passing cars. 'Don't tell anyone, OK?' Perhaps she's forgotten about the holiday to Disneyland she needs me to NOT TALK for! 'Like Mum and Dad. It's nothing, really.'

I shrug my shoulders and she seems a bit happier at that. We carry on walking in silence for a little while longer, and then Susie turns to me with an urgent look on her face. 'Do you know what we learned about in religious studies today, Ant?' she asks.

I mean, where do I start?

Susie plays with the hairband tied around her wrist. 'We learned about Raksha Bandhan,' she ploughs on. 'It's this festival in India. It's where girls tie this sort of sacred thread on the wrist of their brother. It's symbolic and stuff.' She looks at me in earnest. 'It's a mark of mutual love and respect and of always looking out for each other.'

I nod, 'cos she's looking at me expectantly, but to be honest I've no idea what she's banging on about.

Susie trails her feet along the ground as she walks. 'It's just . . .' she starts, and she looks up at the sky as if trying to find the right words. 'Those girls and me. We don't really get on.' In the silence, Susie obviously feels compelled to explain, because she goes on, 'They – they don't think I should be playing Annie when I'm only Year Seven.' She lets out a big puff of air, as if that was the hardest thing she's ever had to say. 'They're just jealous, I suppose,' she sniffs, and I look over to see that she's got tears in her eyes.

Wow. This is unexpected. I've hardly ever seen Susie down. She's always so happy and upbeat it's nauseating. Still. I look over at her, and even though my cheeks ache from all the breaming, I shoot her a smile.

Susie studies my face as we turn into Conway Avenue and head to number twelve, and beams right back. 'Thanks, Ant,' she says, and she finds my hand and gives it a little squeeze. 'I really appreciate this chat.' Then she takes the hairband off her wrist and puts it on mine. Even though she knows I've got really short hair and don't need it and am a boy. 'Just like in India,' she says and laughs. 'We're bound to each other now.'

With that, she skips off up the drive to our house. Honestly. Actors.

Dinner's just about the worst you can get. Not 'cos of the sea bream, which is quite tasty, actually, and worth all the 'Skate! Saxophone! Smile!' shenanigans.

But 'cos Ben's there.

Course he flaming is.

Dad scrapes a chair back for Ben like he's the King of Britain. Dad never scrapes back a chair for any of *us*.

Ben's just about to sit at the table when he picks up a Thomas Cook brochure lying on the seat. It's open at a page saying 'Five-star Stay at Disneyland for Three-star Prices' and someone has helpfully highlighted the page and written 'Just Saying' on it.

Dad frowns at all of us. 'Duly noted,' he says.

There are a million pots and pans in the sink and

Mum's all flustered 'cos she forgot to do the herb sauce for the fish and instead we've got to have salad cream with it. Blah!

Ben just looks at all of us with this huge grin on his face. I think he must be drunk, 'cos Dad keeps giving him beers and Robbie's looking all jealous. Then Ben decides to be TOTALLY ANNOYING and starts dishing out advice to all of us, like Mum's dishing out the green beans.

I pretend I'm not listening, and instead I turn to Lucy and start pulling faces at her. She squeals in delight and I'm pleased that somebody at least is paying attention to me.

This is the sort of nonsense Ben came out with:

To Robbie: 'Don't stress about your GCSEs, mate. You'll do brilliantly. You've just got to study hard, keep your head down, and not get distracted by girls or music. There'll be plenty of time for that later.'

From the corner of my eye, I see Mum mouth, 'THANK YOU!' at him.

To Jacob: 'I can't believe you're in Mensa. You must have got that from your mum's side of the family.' (Dad hoots here like a hyena on laughing gas.) 'You'll be running the country at this rate, Jake. I'd rather trust you with my money than that idiot at Number Ten.' Which is a bit rude, 'cos he doesn't even know our neighbour Mrs Taylor.

To Susie: 'I'll be there in the front row, cheering you on. I might even sing along to "It's the Hard Knock Life". If you're unlucky.'

And then he says: 'You know, when I was growing up, Sid Carney, this kid in my street, stopped talking for about six months. It was just a phase. He grew out of it right enough. He's a motivational speaker now, I think. You can't shut him up.'

It takes me a moment, but I realize he's directing this advice at ME. Me!

'Tight-lipped Tony, hey?' Ben grins at me. Tony? Nobody calls me Tony. Puh-lease.

I busy myself with helping Lucy eat her food, but I catch Dad beam at Ben like he's a miracle worker. I wish he could just miracle his way out of our lives.

Ben looks like the cat that got the cream, which is how Badger sometimes looks when he's lying in the road and can hear a car approaching.

I push my plate away from me and leave the table. 'You not having any cheesecake?' Mum asks me, but I just smile as if to say, 'Thank you for a simply wonderful meal. Even if I had to go and fetch it myself, and it was covered in salad cream, and I had to put up with terrible company, but I can't bear to be here any longer, so I've got to miss out on my favourite dessert after a cheeseboard.'

Honestly. After Lucy was born, Dad said, 'NO MORE KIDS!' like that, to Mum. And yet as soon as he finds out he's got another son, he invites him round our flaming house *all the time*.

But Mum just smiles back at me and I traipse out of the kitchen and upstairs, Ben's stupid voice grating in my ears the whole way.

## Tuesday 1 July

## 8.30 p.m.

I HATE JACOB!!!!!

At this moment in time, I hate him more than Ben!

Mum and Dad kicked off, and said I had to go to bed without any milk and chocolate Hobnobs, and that I wasn't allowed to go on the computer for ONE WEEK, and that I'm not allowed a new comic this weekend.

All because I made Jacob go and sit in the airing cupboard.

I'm sitting on my bed, adding to my OPER-ATION GROB file:

## OPERATION GROB:

- Push Ben out of the window. Pretend there was a very strong gust of wind.
- Tell Mum and Dad about our plan to get to Disneyland, then pretend it was Ben who told them.
- Try and get him abducted by aliens. No, that wouldn't work. They wouldn't want him. They'd probably send him back.

When Jacob comes traipsing into my bedroom — well, technically it's *our* bedroom, but still — he's brought Ben with him. Can't a person get a moment's peace in the comfort of their own bedroom without annoying people who share a dad with you barging in?

I scowl and pretend I'm massively absorbed in my work so I don't have to look at them, but from the corner of my eye I can see what they're up to. Jacob's showing Ben around our room, which takes all of two seconds, 'cos there's just enough space for our two beds, a wardrobe that we have to share, and a chest of drawers underneath the window. Dad says, 'You can't swing a cat in here,' but I reckon Badger would like that 'cos his brains would get all bashed about.

The thing Ben's really here to see, though, is Jacob's telescope.

As well as being a maths whizz and a crossword puzzle brainiac, Jacob's really into astronomy, which is looking at stars and planets and stuff. He spends hours and hours on his own, just looking at the Moon and Mars and the Big Dipper. I think he's seen too much *Doctor Who*.

'Oh wow, mate!' Ben exclaims, and walks to the window, where the telescope's positioned next to the chest of drawers. 'It's a beauty.'

Jacob's beaming with pride and he shows Ben how to adjust the lens and how to swivel the telescope round for optimum observation. Ben puts his eye to the eyepiece and I kick myself then. If I'd known he'd be up here looking at it, I'd have put permanent marker on it and given him a black eye.

The two of them stare up at the stars in silence and

wonder, and I'm wondering when the heck Ben's going to leave. 'You want to have a look, mate?' Ben says to me, taking his eye from the telescope and smiling over.

I don't say anything.

Ben lets out a little sigh and he and Jacob go back to stargazing. After about four hours, Ben checks his big silver watch and says he's got to leave.

About flaming time.

He gives Jacob a little hug, and then heads for the door. As he gets there, he turns back and studies me for a moment. 'Well,' he says to me, 'night then, Ant.'

I just keep my head down and focus on my journal. Eventually, Ben turns away and heads downstairs.

Jacob walks over and flops down on his bed. 'That was rude,' he says softly after a moment.

I shoot him a look. Jacob sort of shrinks back a bit.

'He was only being nice,' he says, adjusting his glasses. 'He says he's going to take us all to the cinema.'

Blah! The last time we went to the cinema it was

to see *The Hobbit: The Desolation of Smaug* for the Button Family Boxing Day Outing. All I wanted was to watch the flaming film, but my family – like always – made that impossible. Robbie was crunching popcorn like an Orc; Susie kept going on about one dwarf's facial expressions and how he clearly wasn't a 'Method' actor, whatever that was, and Jacob had to leave three times to go for a wee, so Dad had to keep getting up and going, 'Excuse me, excuse me,' to everyone in our aisle, and they all kept tutting at us, so in the end Dad and Jacob had to stay out and wait for us by the pick'n'mix.

I still don't say anything, so Jacob leans over and lifts up the cover of my journal so he can see what I'm doing.

I snatch it away like a hot potato. I glower at him, and scribble furiously on a bit of paper,

STOP TOUCHING MY STUFF!!!!!

And I hold up my fist like I'm going to thump him.

Jacob backs away a little bit. 'I know what it's like, you know,' he says softly. 'I saw a psychologist when I was five, remember? To test me for Mensa.'

And he looks at me like he thinks we're the same. So I write:

WE ARE NOT THE SAME. I DON'T WANT TO BE A FREAK LIKE YOU.

Jacob's eyes start to well up, and he opens his mouth like he's going to call out to Mum, so I quickly scribble:

GO AND SIT IN THE AIRING CUPBOARD!!!!

He looks at me in confusion, so I hold it up for him to read again. 'But I can't look at the stars in the airing cupboard,' Jacob whispers.

I shrug my shoulders to show I really don't care, and even though I know it's not the nicest thing I've written, I scrawl:

## YOU ARE SUCH A BRAINY, NERDY, FOUR-EYED FREAK.

It wasn't even anything bad! But Jacob starts snivelling, and then he gets up off the bed and walks out onto the landing and opens the airing cupboard door and squeezes himself inside, right by the boiler. He shuts the door right up, but I can still hear him sniffing away.

I manage to get a little bit of work on OPERATION GROB done, but then Dad pads up the stairs, and before I know it he's at the bedroom door, with Jacob right beside him, shouting: 'Why are you being mean to your brother? For God's sake, Anthony, what is wrong with you!'

And so now I'm not allowed to play *Call of Duty* or anything for a week.

Stupid brothers.

# Wednesday 2 July

Today I am famous and feeling like a slice of Pule. It's totally rare and unique and is made from the milk of Balkan donkeys from Serbia. That's how I feel. Like rare and unique, obviously, not a Balkan donkey.

At school, a few of the other pupils get the idea to not talk so they haven't got to do this stupid presentation either, and they go around copying everything I do.

I first notice it in the playground before registration. Mum drops me off, and as I head over to where Murphy and Lee Foreman are kicking a ball about, a group of girls from 5W come up to me and start giggling. I shoot them a look, as if to say:

'Girls. Please. I haven't got time for your silliness and ridiculousness.'

When I reach Murphy and Lee, I hold up my hand to say, 'Hi!' and beam at both of them. Lee holds up his hand too, but he doesn't say 'Hi!' out loud, and Murphy's acting really strange, as if he didn't see me do it at all. The girls have followed me over and, without saying anything, they hold up their hands to each other too, and wiggle their eyebrows up and down.

Odd.

Assembly's pretty interesting, what with most of Year 5 not talking. When Mrs Tribe, the headmistress, walks to the front of the hall and says, 'Good morning, everybody,' only the pupils in Years 3, 4 and 6 reply. When it comes to singing that morning's hymn, 'One More Step Along the World I Go', it sounds decidedly quiet, and it's pretty clear that Year 5 aren't joining in. Beside my row, I can see Mr Reeve standing there, his arms folded, staring at me with a frown.

As we file back to our classroom and I stop off at

the sink to get a glass of water, Stacy sidles up to me. 'Everyone's copying you,' she whispers. 'With the not talking.'

Everyone except Stacy, obviously.

I sit down at my table, and all through history hour I notice everyone shooting me looks every now and then, and making notes to each other and stuff like that. It's dead quiet in class. Mr Reeve does a lot of huffing and puffing, 'cos he's fed up with no one answering his questions and everyone just shrugging every time he asks someone to read out what answer they put on their 'Triggers of the First World War' worksheet.

At lunch, I'm just about to join Michael and Murphy and Lee, who are playing football over by the nature reserve, when I pass Frankie Mellor sitting quietly near the log seats reading a book. She looks up as I approach and then looks back down at her book again, holding it right up to her nose so she blocks me out. I don't quite know why I do this, but I lean over and pull the book down so she has to look at me.

'Wh-wh-what d-d-d-d-d-d-d-d-do you w-w-w-w-w-want?' she stutters, blushing bright red.

I take my notepad from my back pocket and scribble:

## DUNNO. JUST THOUGHT I'D SAY HELLO.

She reads it and shoots me a withering look. 'Well, s-s-s-s-s-s-s-say it, then,' she mumbles.

She puts her book up again, right in front of her face, and it's pretty obvious she doesn't want to carry on with our little chat. How rude!

Just then I feel a tap on my shoulder, and I spin round to see Samir Stamford grinning at me. 'That was Woody Wattler,' he says, rolling his eyes in Woody Wattler's direction. 'Hello, gang.'

I stumble back a few steps when I realize that Samir's just touched me. Oh God, oh God, please don't let me catch his weirdness.

'I don't think we've been properly introduced,' Samir says matter-of-factly. He sticks out his hand, but Frankie ignores him. 'I'm Samir,' he continues, letting his hand drop back by his side. 'But you can call me Sam. And this is Woody Wattler.' He points to the empty space beside him. 'You can call him Woody Wattler.' And he throws his head back and laughs like the lunatic he is.

Frankie lets out a sigh and peers out from behind her book. 'L-l-l-l-l-l-look,' she states and then she stops and takes a couple of deep breaths. 'I d-d-d-d-d-don't w-w-w-w-want.' She bites her lip. More deep breaths. 'W-w-w-w-w-w-we're n-n-n-n-n-not . . .' she stammers and her face is bright red. She lets out a sigh of frustration and snatches my notepad from me.

Before I can call out 'Hey!' even if I wanted to, she scribbles something down and shoves the pad back at me.

'*Just because we all go to the same shrink doesn't make us friends,*' Samir reads out over my shoulder.

Frankie shoves her book inside her bag and storms off the logs and across the playground.

'Well, there's no need to be so rude,' Samir calls after her. He shakes his head in disbelief and trots off to the climbing frame, chatting to Woody Wattler all the while.

This school is downright bonkers.

I head over to the nature reserve, pull off my jumper and shove it on the pile of goalposts. I go to tackle Lee, but instead Murphy blocks my way. He's not said a word to me all morning, but I didn't mind 'cos I just thought he was copying me too.

Murphy stoops down and picks up the football. With a scowl on his face, he hisses, 'Nobody likes a show-off.'

I'm too shocked to scribble anything down. Why's he being all moody? Just as I'm closing my mouth in surprise, he's off again, running after Michael Hadley. He slings his arm around Michael's shoulders, being all friendly, and he turns and looks back at me with a smirk on his face.

Things are equally less brilliant in the afternoon. Mr Reeve cottons on to why everyone's not talking and he blames me! *Me!*

We're all sat on the carpet ready for afternoon

registration, and Mr Reeve's getting more and more huffy and puffy. It goes like this:

MR REEVE: Good afternoon, Rashid.

RASHID:

> *Mr Reeve frowns, but looks up, spots Rashid, and puts a mark by his name.*

MR REEVE: Good afternoon, Stephanie.

STEPHANIE:

> *Mr Reeve frowns again, but puts a 1 by Stephanie's name.*

MR REEVE: Good afternoon, James.

JAMES:

> *Jemima, Amy and Lauren giggle at the back.*

MR REEVE: What is going on?

CLASS 5R:

MR REEVE: Huff, huff, huff. Good afternoon, Meadow.

MEADOW: Good afternoon, Mr Reeve.

> *Class 5R shoot Meadow a look. She's such a goody-goody.*

MR REEVE: Thank you, Meadow. Good afternoon, Jemima.

JEMIMA:

**MR REEVE:** Cat got your tongue, Jemima?

**JEMIMA:**

**MR REEVE:** Huff, Huff, Huff. Good afternoon, Roxy.

**ROXY:**

**MR REEVE:** Oh, for goodness' sake. Would someone kindly explain to me why nobody is talking today?

**CLASS 5R:**

So, that was fun for about three minutes, until Mr Reeve snaps the register shut. 'Anthony,' he says, glowering, 'do you know why the whole of 5R have stopped talking?'

'Uh,' Meadow goes.

'The whole of 5R except Meadow Jenkins,' Mr Reeve corrects.

Everyone's looking at me like I'm the leader of all the not-talking people. I shrug my shoulders. Mr Reeve stares at all of us firmly. 'If nobody explains to me why you are all silent,' he says slowly, 'then I've no choice but to keep you all behind after school.'

Everyone looks at one another. You can tell he's got them there.

Jemima's the first to fold. Honestly, she'd make a rubbish spy. 'I've got a riding lesson after school,' she says, sticking out her chin.

'Well, I suggest you start talking,' Mr Reeve replies.

Jemima lets out a sigh, looks to Amy and Lauren, who give her a nod, and says, 'None of us are talking so we won't have to do the presentation.'

Mr Reeve's eyebrows shoot upwards. 'What do you mean?'

'Anthony's getting out of it by not talking. So we all thought we would too.'

Mr Reeve looks very hard at me again and folds his arms. 'If Anthony Button thinks he's getting out of the presentation by not talking, he's got another think coming.'

Everyone goes, 'Oooooooooh,' at that, like they're expecting it to kick off.

'This presentation *will* be going ahead,' Mr Reeve continues, 'and EVERYONE will be taking part.' He looks around at the class then, and everyone seems to shuffle back a bit on the carpet. 'No exceptions.' He clears his throat and looks like he's had a brainwave. 'Even if you all have to do it in mime, or Powerpoint or through interpretive dance.'

'That I'd like to see,' Mrs Wintour pipes up from the back of the room, where she's guillotining our display work.

Everyone starts moaning to each other then and rolling their eyes and going, 'Oh, miss, it's not fair,' and, 'Please, Mr Reeve, we don't want to do it.'

Mr Reeve's having none of it, and he gives me this little smirk like he's won this round.

But I'm not too disheartened. 'Cos even though I've got to do this flaming presentation after all, one thing's for sure – I'm better than ALL my classmates at this not-talking malarkey. Everyone caved in after less than a day and I've been going for six whole days now. This *is* my thing! Maybe I should start a website.

# Wednesday 2 July

## 7 p.m.

I'm lying on my bed making a list of all the things I can do to get out of this flaming presentation. All right, I've discovered I'm better than everyone in my class at Not Talking, but standing up in front of the whole of Year 5 and their families – and my family – trying to act out the word 'Badger'? No thanks.

### MY FAMILY AND OTHER ANIMALS

- Write a brochure for people to read, like when you go to the pantomime and buy a programme.

- Write the presentation and pay someone to read it.

- Pretend you're about to do the presentation, but then fake a heart attack and get carted off stage so you can't do it. (This may be a bit mean for Mum and Dad to have to watch, though – they might freak out. And I'm not that good an actor.)

- Pay the local zoo to release a swarm of frogs into the hall just as I'm about to come on, meaning everyone has to get up and leave for fear of being croaked on.

- Pay someone to set off the fire alarm just as I'm about to do my presentation. Hmm, the only person I know gutsy enough to do this is Murphy, and he's being a bit funny with me at the moment.

Most of these suggestions involve paying someone. Which involves money. Which I haven't got. And I don't know if Bristol Zoo even has any frogs. Blah!

Suddenly the sound of screeching guitars

accompanied by Robbie and his mates belting out some lyrics wash over me.

For God's sake. The noise of them thrashing out the same old song in the garage is drifting upwards and hurting my ears. 'Cos they keep getting it wrong. I mean, how hard can it be? It's just one song. And one line gets repeated over and over again throughout. And *still* they manage to mess it up. It's '*can*', you idiots, not 'could', I almost shout as they get it wrong YET AGAIN! No chance of Robbie and his band standing in any halls, or corridors or cupboards-under-the-stairs, of Fame at this rate. Geez. Even I can get the words right and I don't even *like* The Script.

I've had just about enough of this. I rip a page out of my notepad and storm downstairs.

You have to go through the kitchen to get to the 'music room' which was once the garage, and Robbie's put loads of signs on the door, like: BORN TO ROCK! and BEWARE: MUSICAL GENIUS AT WORK.

I burst through the door, holding up my piece

of paper. Robbie stops playing his guitar as soon as he sees me; Smithy stops banging on the drums and Mark stops bashing away at the keyboard. The song comes crashing to a halt as everyone peers at my piece of paper. It says:

IF YOU INSIST ON PLAYING THE SAME SONG OVER AND OVER AND OVER AGAIN, AT LEAST GET THE FLAMING WORDS RIGHT.

I think I get my point across, because Robbie frowns and says, 'Oh, yeah? What should it be, then?'

I quickly scribble:

CAN. STANDING. GONNA. NOT COULD, LIVING OR GONNA.

Honestly. What would will.i.am make of this shambles? I think for a moment, and add:

AND THE DRUMMER'S HALF A SECOND LATE ON EVERY BEAT.

Robbie shakes his plectrum at Smithy. 'I told you!' he yells, and then he beams right at me. 'Thanks, Ant. Hey, you wanna stay and watch us for a little bit?'

Well, that's a first. Normally if anyone dares to poke their head round the garage door, Robbie screams blue flaming murder at us and moans that Paul McCartney never had to put up with such interruptions when rehearsing with The Beatles. We all think Robbie's aiming a little *too* high with that comparison, but still. He's never invited me to watch them before.

So I sit down on the edge of Robbie's bed, and as they strike up the opening chords of 'Hall of Fame' for the seventeenth time today I nod along in time to the rhythm and Robbie grins as he sings the lyrics – the *right* lyrics – at me.

I feel like a right groupie.

And I quite like it, truth be told.

# Thursday 3 July

Today I am feeling like an Époisses.
It's 'highly pungent' with an 'overwhelmingly sweet aroma'
and I'm feeling a bit overwhelmed today. But not by sweet
aromas, 'cos Mum hasn't cleaned.

It's my second appointment with Jess today. I sit down on the chair next to her, and notice all the paintings hanging on the walls. Hand-drawn pictures of houses and football pitches and boats, like they've been drawn by kids. I think they might be from all her other case studies. In the centre of the wall is a framed picture of a quote which says:

> *At the core of ethics: a command that one try*
> *to imagine what it might be like to be someone else.*
> *Alain de Botton*

I don't know what it means, but it's in fancy writing, so it must be clever.

I get my pen and my Transformers notepad ready in case Jess wants to do another word association game, but instead she whacks a lump of Play-Doh on her desk and says, 'Let's create feelings characters.'

I mean, where do I start?

'No?' Jess asks, catching the look on my face. 'OK, well, what about this?' And she pulls from a drawer a piece of card with a wheel of cheese on it. A WHEEL OF CHEESE! It's basically a big circle divided into eight segments with a different cheese in each bit.

'When your dad and me had a little chat the other day,' Jess says, 'I asked him what sort of things you were into. He said cheese.'

Well, what can I say? All right, no one's seen

my list of stuff that could potentially be MY THING, but seriously, is that ALL Dad could think of?

THINGS I LIKE
- DOCTOR WHO
- JAMES BOND
- ALIENS
- COMICS
- JOKES. LIKE: 'Does an apple a day keep the doctor away? Yes, if you aim it well enough.' NOT: 'Well, I'll Brie damned.'
- FOOTBALL. AT LEAST I DID TILL BEN SAID HE LIKED IT SO MUCH
- YES, ALL RIGHT. CHEESE

So a wheel of cheese it was. Jess said I had to point to the cheese I most felt like when she gave me a scenario. Like:

JESS: You're late for school.
ME: *Points to a Cheddar*

| JESS: | You got told off at school. |
| ME: | *Points to a Stilton* |
| JESS: | Your mum tells you off. |
| ME: | *Points to a Stilton* |
| JESS: | You score a goal in a football match. |
| ME: | *Points to a Red Leicester* |

And so on and so on. It got a bit boring after a while 'cos the wheel didn't even have any good cheeses, like Double Gloucester or Flosserkäse, so I just pointed at whatever was nearest. But Jess said it's good to explore negative emotions and that there's nothing wrong with showing when you're angry or upset, 'cos they're not 'bad' emotions. Which I guess *is* easier to explore through Play-Doh than pointing.

Before I knew it, our half-hour was up. It was what happened after that was weirder than a purple beard-o.

I head out of Jess's office and into reception, thinking about the pizza I'm going to have when Dad takes me out for a 'light bite' again, when all of a sudden a woman in a suit, with black bobbed hair, stands up and greets me.

'Hello, Anthony,' she says. 'I'm Samir's mother. I thought you might like to come round for dinner tonight. Your dad's agreed.'

Dad smiles encouragingly at me. 'Sounds good, doesn't it, Ant?' he says.

NO! I frown at him. It's definitely my best ever frowning. IT SOUNDS TERRIBLE! God knows what sort of weirdness I could catch at his ACTUAL HOUSE!

'Might do you good to spend time with a kindred spirit,' Dad says, and he leans over and ruffles my hair. 'Mrs Stamford will drop you off at ours after tea.' And then he shakes Samir's mum's hand, and heads off across reception. CLACK CLACK CLACK.

'Samir's in with Dr Hiddleston at the moment,' Samir's mum says. She sits back down on the chair and takes her BlackBerry out of her pocket. 'He'll not be long. There's plenty of magazines.' And she starts tapping away on her phone while I sink into a chair as all thoughts of pizza with Dad drift from my mind.

## SAM HAS NOT ONE, BUT TWO XBOXES!!!

They're both his! Well, one's for Sam and one's for Woody Wattler, but seeing as Woody Wattler DOESN'T EXIST they're both his! We've only got one between the seven of us at home. Some people have all the luck.

Sam's house is dead posh. It's detached, which means he doesn't have any neighbours, and it's got four bedrooms. We've only got three and a converted garage!

Sam leads me upstairs to his room and I make sure I keep a good distance behind him. Sam's got a Blu-ray DVD player and a plasma screen TV and two Teenage Mutant Ninja Turtles bean bags in front of the TV. And he has a double bed in his room, and blue curtains, and a Teenage Mutant Ninja Turtles duvet and Teenage Mutant Ninja Turtles wallpaper. I think he likes Teenage Mutant Ninja Turtles.

We slump into the bean bags and I tuck my hands under my bum so I don't touch him. 'Wanna play Xbox?' Samir asks.

Ha! Silly old Dad can't ban me from playing Xbox at Sam's house, can he? He's the one who sent me here in the first place.

I nod and Samir's face lights up. 'Excellent!' he says. 'Sometimes all I want is someone to play Xbox with. Woody Wattler's no good at it.'

I take my notepad out of my pocket and scribble:

## WHY HAVE YOU GOT TWO XBOXES?

Samir peers at my writing, then says, 'Actually, I've got four. Two sets here at Mum's house, two sets of everything at my dad's.'

I stare at him in disbelief. Four?

'I spend three nights a week at Dad's house, and the rest of the time here,' Samir explains. 'Mum and Dad both want to make sure I have everything I need.'

So me and Samir play *Call of Duty* for forty whole minutes, which is totally ace because I only ever get to play for about five minutes in our house before annoying siblings grab the controls.

Just before we're called for dinner, Samir nips to the loo and while he's there I spot on his bed something familiar. Well, all right, it's not *on* his bed, it's under his pillow. Under two pillows, right over the other side of the bed, shoved down pretty deep, but still. It's got PROPERTY OF written on the front and PERSONAL DETAILS on the first page. Jess must have given Sam a journal too, just like this one.

I'll be honest: I'm tempted. I could just flip it open to any page and read how purple beard-o Samir really is, 'cos he's bound to have written down stuff about Woody Wattler. About why he even made Woody Wattler up. Why would anyone even *have* an imaginary friend?

But I can't do it. 'Cos I think about how I'd feel if anyone dared to read *my* journal. Can you imagine how purple beard-o they'd think *I* was, with all my feelings about cheese and OPERATION GROB and everything? No. It's tempting to read it, but I can't, 'cos that's mean and *I* wouldn't like it. Wasn't that what Jess's quote on the wall meant? *Imagine what it's like to be someone else?* So, as I hear the toilet flush next door, I shove the journal back under the pillow and saunter out onto the landing, pretty pleased with myself for being such a nice and decent human being.

We have mushroom risotto for dinner, which I'd never even heard of before. It's basically like rice with bits of mushroom in, and I even ate the handful of broccoli Samir's nanny served with it.

That's right. Nanny. A broccoli-serving nanny.

Samir's mum was busy working in her office, so Samir has this woman who comes in on the nights he's staying there and cooks his dinner for him. Imagine having your own chef! She cooks whatever Samir wants. It's like staying at The Ritz!

If I had my own chef, I would have:

## MONDAY:

Breakfast   Cheese on toast

Lunch      2 slices of homemade cheesecake

Dinner    Mushroom risotto

## TUESDAY:

Breakfast   Bacon sandwich

Lunch      Cheese and onion crisps, with doorstep Red
Leicester sandwiches

Dinner    4-cheese pizza

## WEDNESDAY:

Breakfast   4-cheese pizza. And my chef would make a fresh
one for me, I wouldn't just eat last night's leftovers,
like Dad does sometimes with leftover Chinese

Lunch      Cheesecake

Dinner    Chicken korma with pilau rice and a garlic naan,
just to mix things up a bit

## THURSDAY:

Breakfast   Rice Krispies. I might give my chef the day off – I
can make those myself

Lunch      A whole wheel of Dairylea triangles

Dinner    Macaroni cheese

## FRIDAY:

| | |
|---|---|
| Breakfast | Cheese on toast |
| Lunch | Sausage sandwich |
| Dinner | Fish and chips, 'cos it would be Fish-and-Chips Friday |

## SATURDAY:

| | |
|---|---|
| Breakfast | Cheese on toast |
| Lunch | A Sunday lunch for lunch, even though it's not Sunday! Just 'cos my chef would have to do it if I made her. That is power! |
| Dinner | Pick 'n' mix |

## SUNDAY:

| | |
|---|---|
| Breakfast | Cheese on toast |
| Lunch | Sunday lunch again, 'cos I really like them. And it's a Sunday, so I think it's actually the law that you have to have one |
| Dinner | Cheeseboard |

Samir's got a pretty sweet life, that's for sure. Imagine the peace and quiet! No Robbie or Susie or Jacob or Lucy or Mum or Dad to be simply and utterly ANNOYING all day every day. And —

No Ben!

NO BEN!!!

What a sweeeeet life.

# Thursday 3 July

## 7.10 p.m.

After dinner, Samir's mum drives me home, like she promised Dad she would. The car's black and sleek, like a limo. I feel like a celebrity.

My whole family are in the front garden. Susie, Mum and Lucy are holding hands and prancing round in circles, going 'Ring-a-ring o' roses, a pocket full of posies' like right geeks, truth be told. Robbie's sat on a deckchair, strumming his guitar, and Dad's next to him, ordering him to play a song called 'Why Does It Always Rain on Me?' by Travis. Dad's got a beer in his hand, but I don't think it's his first. And right there, on a deckchair next to them, is Ben.

OF COURSE HE'S FLAMING THERE, JUST
LIKE HE ALWAYS IS!!!

Oh, wait – Jacob's not in the front garden. He's
leaning out of our bedroom window, his telescope
pointing up to the sky. Badger's on the windowsill
next to him, teetering a *little* too close to the edge.

Next to me Samir inhales sharply. 'Oh. My. God,'
he whispers.

I look over to Samir with a tight smile on my
face, which I'm hoping says, 'I'm really sorry you
have to see this, Samir. We've just come from your
lovely, normal house to what I can only describe as
being like a day trip to the safari park – you know,
where you get to hang out with the baboons.'

'Cos obviously Samir thinks my family are a
bunch of peculiars. And therefore *I* am a peculiar.
Not that I should be bothered about what Samir
thinks, what with him being king of the peculiars,
but still.

'Are they always like this?' Samir says.

I shrug my shoulders, as if to say, 'What can you
do? You can't choose your family, hey?'

But Samir just grins back at me. Positively BREAMS. 'Your family are brilliant!'

WHAAAAAAAA?

'I know, Woody,' Samir's saying. 'Shambolic, but brilliant.'

Shambolic? Yes. Brilliant? No.

Having fun while I'm not there? Yes. Having fun *because* I'm not there? Most definitely probably yes.

Hmph.

I smile politely at Mrs Stamford, then climb out of the car. Mum gets up off the ground from where she and Susie and Lucy have collapsed in a heap after the millionth 'WE ALL FALL DOWN' and waves to Samir and Mrs Stamford as she reverses the car out of the drive. Dad's too busy laughing with Ben and opening another bottle of beer.

'Did you have fun, love?' Mum beams at me. 'What did you have for dinner?'

I don't reply in any way, and as I walk past everyone to the front door I can see Mum shooting Dad a look. Dad sighs, and as I head into the porch I hear him clattering about, putting down his beer and getting up out of the chair. I can tell he's doing that, 'cos he always makes this 'OOF' sound whenever he gets up out of chairs, usually followed by, 'Ooh, me knees.'

I head upstairs, and I've barely had time to drop my rucksack, flop down on my bed and totally ignore Jacob when Dad's at the bedroom door, peering down at me.

'Anthony, my boy,' he booms, and he sweeps into the room and sits down on the bed. 'Everything all right?'

Dad looks at me curiously, then peers over to Jacob, who's still half hanging out of the window. 'Jacob, mate. Can you give us a moment?'

Jacob sighs, puts down his notepad and scuttles out of the room, Badger trotting after him. Jacob gives me a little smile as he leaves, but I'm too busy frowning at Dad to do anything about it.

'Everything all right at Sam's house?'

I shrug my shoulders as if to say, 'Yeah, and? So he's got two Xboxes and a chef. What about it?'

I think Dad gets it, 'cos he bites his lip, then says, 'Sorry we didn't go out for pizza like I said we would after you see Dr Morley.'

Hmph. If he was that sorry, he wouldn't have packed me off to Samir's house in the first place, mushroom risotto or no mushroom risotto.

Dad leans in to whisper to me almost conspiratorially, 'I'll let you have two slices of pizza next time to make up for it. Just don't tell your mother.' He gives a little laugh, and he pats me on the knee. 'All right?'

At least he's trying, I suppose.

'Incidentally, your mum and me,' Dad continues, 'we're really looking forward to this presentation of yours, you know.'

Blah! I'd forgotten about that.

'"My Family and Other Animals", hey?' Dad says, shooting me a grin. 'I bet you've got enough material about us to write a whole book.'

I can't help it. Before I know what I'm doing, I'm smiling right back at him.

Dad seems to perk up a bit at that. 'If you need

any help with anything on it, you just let me know,' he beams.

There's footsteps on the stairs then, and Dad turns round to see who's on the landing. 'Ah!' he says as Ben appears at the bedroom door, holding a cardboard box. 'Maybe you could help too?'

'With what?' Ben asks.

'Anthony's presentation. You do a lot of presentations for work, don't you? Perhaps you could give him some tips.'

Ben grins at me. 'I'd love to,' he replies.

Would you now? I think. Well, nobody asked you. I mean, Dad just did, obviously, but I VERY MUCH didn't.

Dad gets up off the bed. 'Oof, me knees,' he goes. He does that when getting up off beds too. And out of car seats. And up off cinema seats. And off roller-coaster seats. Anything involving sitting down to standing up, really. 'Come on, then.' Dad nods to Ben, and before I know it Ben's scooting through the door and hovering alongside my bed. 'I'll leave you to it,' Dad says and saunters downstairs.

Ben continues to hover at my bedside, clearly unsure as to whether he should sit down at the end of my bed or not. 'VERY MUCH *OR NOT*, BEN,' I silently scream at him from inside my brain.

He has a lot of faults, does Ben, and now he can add not being psychic to them because, balancing the cardboard box on his knee, he sits right down on the edge of my bed like he actually *belongs* here. 'Your mum did already tell me about your presentation,' he says, looking at me sort of shyly. 'So, I thought you could use this.' From his pocket he pulls out a photograph. It's of a lanky kid with brown hair and a big nose, wearing a Bristol Rovers football kit, grinning cheesily into the camera. The kid can't be more than seven or eight.

Ben holds out the photograph. 'It's me,' he says softly. 'When I was your age.'

Well, how stupid can one person be? That kid's Jacob's age, not mine!

I reach down the side of the bed and drag my rucksack up. I take out my Transformers notepad and pen and scribble on a new page:

# I'M 10!!!

Ben grins at me sheepishly. 'Even so. You can have it. For your presentation.' I don't take the photograph from him, so after a moment Ben pops it on top of my rucksack. He clears his throat. 'Seeing as it's about family, and everything.'

'YOU'RE NOT FAMILY!!!' I scream at him silently inside my head. Then I remember how rubbish and unpsychic he is. So I frown at him again. It's definitely my best ever frowning.

'If you need to talk about family traits,' he ploughs on, too stupid to notice I'm narrowing my eyes at him, 'I've always loved football. Always. Football crazy and football mad me.'

He grins again shyly. His cheeks look a bit flushed, as if he's been running. 'I've got a match next Thursday, in fact, at Furton Park. The tenth. A big match.' He clears his throat again. 'There's someone important coming too. A talent scout. From Reading . . .'

I'm still doing some excellent frowning at him.

'I'm quite nervous about it, actually,' he says softly, more to himself than me. 'Not told anyone else about it yet, in fact. Well, Mum knows. Dad doesn't. Yet.'

Is that true, IN FACT? Holy Moly! I want to shout, 'STOP BORING ME!' I want to shout, 'JUST LEAVE ME ALONE! GET OUT OF MY ROOM AND STOP GOING ON ABOUT FOOTBALL!' 'Cos I'm annoyed that I can't even have football as a hobby now, what with Ben being so flaming ace at it.

But then a genius thought pops into my head. I think of how perfect it would be for OPERATION GROB.

I grab my notepad and quickly scrawl:

I'LL TELL DAD IF YOU'RE NERVOUS ABOUT IT.

Ben's face breaks out into a smile so bright you could light the whole of Wiltshire with it.

'Really?' he says. 'Oh, wow. Wow! Thanks, Ant. That would be great. Yeah, I have been a bit nervous. Thanks.'

I smile, and add:

## SURE. LEAVE IT WITH ME.

Ben gets up off the bed, and runs a hand through his hair. 'I really appreciate it,' he says, like the fool that he is. 'You can have that. Really,' he says, pointing at his stupid photo cluttering up my rucksack. 'I don't mind. Seeing as we're family and everything. Oh, almost forgot,' and he gestures to the cardboard box on the bed. 'A present for you. It's a wheel of cheese.'

Honestly. Who tells someone what their present is *before* they open it? I mean, I know Mum did at Christmas with the whole 'Shopping list on the loo roll' incident, but that was an *accident*!

'I'll just leave it here,' Ben says, then plonks the box down on the chest of drawers. 'Great chatting, Ant.' He heads to the door, flashes me one last grin and saunters back downstairs.

I pick up the photo and throw it after him, but 'cos it's just a photo and I'm not really in the mood for throwing, it doesn't get very far and just flutters down on the bed next to me.

I lie down and scrunch my eyes tight shut. My head's swimming, trying to take everything in: Ben swanning in here like he owns the place, talking about football scouts and family. *My* family.

I can hear them through the open window, the sound of their laughing and cackling and rabbiting-on drifting up from the front garden and reaching my ears. I wish I could scrunch those up too. Block out the sound of everyone laughing and joking downstairs. Without me.

I open my eyes and sit bolt upright. OPERATION GROB is a go! If Ben thinks Dad's coming to his stupid match, he's got another think coming. 'Cos the tenth is my presentation, and if I've got to do it then Dad can flaming well come to watch *me*, 'cos I've been in his family for ten whole *years* while Ben's only been in it for ten stupid *days*. He's not taking Dad away from watching me to watch his football match. Maybe Ben will think Dad doesn't care about him so he'll stop coming round and leave us alone!

Result!

I take my pen and add to my list:

## THINGS THAT COULD BE 'MY THING'
- CIRCUS SIDESHOW ACT
- SPY & ASSASSIN
- NINJA
- POLITICIAN, 'COS DAD SAYS THEY'RE ALWAYS DOING SNEAKY THINGS
- EVIL GENIUS. MUCH MORE SUITED TO MY SKILLS

*Mwah-ha-ha.* That's how evil geniuses go in films. I'm just like that, but I'm not really that evil, I'm just doing what's right.

While I've got my pen, I pick up Ben's stupid old photo from my rucksack, and before I can really and truly know what I'm doing I'm scribbling all over it.

See how he likes that! *Mwah-ha-ha!*

I draw a funny moustache on his stupid face, one that's all twirly at the ends, like a proper film villain. Then I draw two devil's horns coming out the top of his head. And I draw a big bubble coming out of Ben's mouth and write in it:

MY NAME IS BEN AND I AM A LOOOOOOOOSER!

I think for a moment and add:

NO ONE LOVES ME.

And then I think for another moment and add:

AND I HAVEN'T GOT A REAL FAMILY OF MY OWN SO THAT'S WHY I HAVE TO GO ROUND STEALING OTHER PEOPLE'S.

I laugh to myself, silently, just shaking my shoulders, and then I fold the photograph in half and shove it inside this journal.

It's true, you know. You can't go round stealing

other people's families. It's not my fault Ben grew up with just his mum, but he doesn't have to keep coming round here all the time. There's no room for him. And not just 'cos we only live in a house with three bedrooms and a garage.

There's no room for him with Mum and Dad. They've got their own kids they need to look after and think about and care for. They haven't got the time or the patience for someone else to come waltzing along, looking for love too. Their love's already got to be shared five ways as it is. Ben can't have the last bit of their love like he had the last bit of Wensleydale.

There's just no room for him. That's all there is to it.

## Friday 4 July

Today I am a limburger. It's a cheese,
not a burger. It's one of the least popular
cheeses ever. Like me. Except I'm
not a cheese, obviously.
But I am unpopular.

'MUTANT! YOU'RE A MUTANT! LOOK AT THE MUTANT, EVERYONE!'

The words are still ringing in my ears.

This morning in class we had to work on our presentation, and I could see Mr Reeve shooting me looks now and then 'cos I was just writing this instead of thinking about family traits:

Q.    What type of cheese is made backwards?
A.    Edam.
Get it? MADE backwards is EDAM!
I'm not being funny, but maybe I should get Mum and Dad to
test me for Mensa too.

Murphy didn't say anything to me the whole morning, even though we sat opposite each other on Saturn table like always. Stacy kept trying to get me to show her what I was working on, but I curled my arm round the top of my journal so no one could see.

Then when Mr Reeve stepped out of the classroom to have a quick word with Miss Watson, out of nowhere Murphy looks at me and says, 'When are you going to start talking again?' Just like that.

Stacy shoots him a look. 'Don't go on at him,' she hisses.

'Don't you think it's a bit stupid?' Murphy huffs.

I just shrug my shoulders.

So then Murphy starts singing, 'Ant-Knee Button

is such a weirdo. Weirder than a purple beard-o!' under his breath.

'Shut up!' Stacy says, but Murphy gives me this horrible smirk. Then Mr Reeve walks back into the classroom, so he sticks his head in his exercise book and pretends he's working really hard.

The bell rings for lunch and I can't wait to get out of the classroom. I scrape back my chair and race over to the cloakroom we share with 5W to pick up my lunch box, and who should already be in there but Samir Stamford.

'Hi, Ant,' Samir beams. 'All right?'

I nod at him, and Samir goes to say something else, when all of a sudden Murphy and Michael Hadley are right next to me, even though they both have hot dinners and don't need to be in here.

'Careful,' Murphy smirks. 'You don't want to catch his purple beardo-ness.'

I grab my lunch box and am about to head out the door when Samir pipes up, 'That's not even a word. Beard-o-ness. Do you mean beardedness?'

Murphy looks at Samir like he's got two heads. Then he turns to me. 'See what I mean?'

Before I can do anything, Samir says, 'Let me know if you want to come over for dinner again, Anthony.'

I freeze in my tracks. I was hoping nobody would ever find out about that.

'WHAT?' Murphy goes, his jaw practically hitting the floor. Michael Hadley giggles next to him.

'Not that it's any of your business, but Anthony came over to mine for dinner yesterday,' Samir says matter-of-factly. 'We played *Call of Duty* and had mushroom risotto and I let Anthony sit in my best Teenage Mutant Ninja Turtles bean bag. Right, Woody Wattler's starving, so we're heading into the hall.' And he breezes out of the cloakroom like the most normal thing in the world has just happened.

'You went to his *house*?' Murphy says to me, his eyes wide.

I try and shrug as casually as I can, but 'cos I'm so nervous it just looks like I've got terrible cramp in my shoulders.

'Have you lost it?' Murphy ploughs on.

'Why would you do that?' Michael Hadley chips in.

'Teenage Mutant Ninja Turtles?' Lee Foreman pipes up, but everyone ignores him.

'I know,' Murphy hisses. 'It's 'cos Ant really *is* as purple beard-o as Samir. Isn't that right?'

'Yeah, I reckon.' Michael Hadley grins.

I stare down at the floor. I know my face is going bright red.

'I bet he likes Teenage Mutant Ninja Turtles too,' Murphy smirks. And then his eyes flash as a thought occurs to him. 'Oh my God. Mutant. He's a Mutant! Get it? Mute-Ant. Oh my God, that's the best thing ever.' And he's pointing at me now, and yelling, 'MUTANT! MUTANT! LOOK AT THE MUTANT, EVERYONE!' over and over again, and before I know it the whole of 5R and 5W are in the cloakroom, picking up their lunch things and they're all laughing at the name.

I feel the hairs on the back of my neck stand up with every cry.

'MUTANT! HE'S A MUTANT!'

My palms are sweaty. My head feels all dizzy.

'MUTANT!'

'It's pretty clever, isn't it?' Murphy yells to the class, performing to the audience. "Cos you're called Ant, and you're not talking. You're a mute. Mute Ant.'

'Shut up,' Stacy yells. 'You're meant to be his friend.'

Murphy's lip curls into a snarl. 'You've got new friends now, haven't you, Mutant? Samir Stamford and his imaginary pal are waiting for you.' He slings his arm round Michael Hadley's shoulders. 'Come on, Michael, I'll go in goal.'

And the pair of them barge past me out of the cloakroom.

Stacy gives me a little smile. 'Just ignore him, Anthony,' she says. 'He's an idiot.' She picks up her lunch box and waltzes out of the door.

When it's just me left, I wipe the back of my sleeve across my eyes. Don't cry, I think to myself. Don't let it get to you. But how could it not? How can your supposed best friend calling you a mutant and making everyone laugh at you not hurt?

I tuck my lunch box under my arm. Just as I'm about to head out into the hall, I feel a hand on my shoulder. I spin round and see Mr Reeve peering down on me. That's all I need.

I start to take my notepad from my pocket and write:

## WHAT HAVE I DONE NOW??

'Cos he's bound to be telling me off for something, like mixing up the paints, or not tucking in my shirt, or for flicking Blu-tack at Jemima during reading time. And I only did *two* of those things today.

But instead he smiles down at me. Actually smiles. And says, 'Do you know something, Anthony? I admire your willpower.' I'm obviously looking confused and not really understanding what 'willpower' is, 'cos he goes on, 'The way you've stuck to your guns with not talking. It certainly takes a strong will to do something like that. Or stubbornness,' he adds with a knowing smile.

I don't say anything. Not just 'cos I'm not talking anyway, but 'cos I don't really know what's going on.

'I could learn a lesson from you about willpower, you know, especially when it comes to chocolate.' Mr Reeve breaks into a full-on grin, then squats down a bit so our faces are level. 'Some of the other children are a little confused about what you're doing,' he says softly, 'and sometimes when people don't understand why a person does something, they lash out and they say mean things.' He smiles down kindly on me. 'I think this could be a wonderful opportunity for you to apply yourself, Anthony,' he says. 'You're a very smart boy and, as we've seen, very determined. So why don't you give yourself a chance and try a little bit harder, hey? I know you'll have some fantastic ideas about your family presentation and about presenting them in a really creative and interesting way. Right?'

I swear this flaming presentation is going to be the death of me. Still. Mr Reeve's looking so earnestly at me, like he thinks this little pep talk makes everything all right, that I feel mean if I don't nod along. So I give him a big smile and his face lights up.

'Wonderful,' he says. 'Now, run along to lunch. I don't want to hold up your daily intake of cheese.' He reaches back to the table behind him and grabs a coffee cup. 'And I have an appointment with a latte.' With that he heads out of the cloakroom and off down the corridor to the staff room.

Sometimes I think I'm the only sane person in this school.

We had a creative writing session after afternoon registration and Mr Reeve said he was going to try something new and 'mix it up a bit', just like I did by having my imaginary chef cook me a curry on Wednesdays. So Mr Reeve moved lots of people around and instead of sitting next to Murphy, like I normally do, I ended up on Jupiter table with Jemima and Rashid, and Stacy joined us too.

Mr Reeve said we could write a story about anything, and that there should be no limits to our imagination. He's always saying that, is Mr Reeve.

'No limits to your imagination, 5R!' he says, and: 'Dare to dream big! What the mind can conceive, the mind can achieve,' and all that sort of thing. So Rashid wrote a story about a spy who's really an alien and I didn't even tell him off for copying *Men in Black*. Jemima wrote about horses, and Stacy wrote about a girl who has to look after her little sister when her mum goes off to the pub.

I thought long and hard about how I could stop being a Limburger cheese. This is my story:

*'The Boy Who Doesn't Want to Be a Limburger Cheese.'*
*by Anthony Button, Class 5R*

Once there was a boy who didn't have as many friends as he wanted, so one day he sat down and made a list of all the things he could do to make new friends. He realized he liked making lists, just like his mum did. Maybe that's a family trait. He should make a note of that. And the boy thought it was very nice to be able to do some work without people calling him a purple beard-o, or mutant, or bothering him with facts about the rings of Saturn, or telling you that the jumper you're wearing is four years old and they wore it so much better when they were your size and, actually, no one wears McFly jumpers any more. The boy's list went:

1. *Run away to the circus and train as a trapeze artist.* Everyone would think I was well good. And it'd probably be quieter than living at home. And I'm used to living with 'animals'.

2. *Live in a cave.* Not in, like, a caveman way, but 'cos you can grow cheese in a cave. I'd be a connoisseur, which is someone who knows their onions about cheese. And I'd discover a totally new cheese and become famous and rich.

3. *Become a blind taster.* Not as in make myself blind and then eat food, but as in: I could wear a blindfold and tell people which cheese was which, 'cos I know four hundred and three different varieties. Fact: in olden days, in medieval England, the King would make someone eat his food first to check it hadn't been poisoned. (If it had, their face would go as red as a fire engine and then their head would explode and their tongue would fall out.) I'd be good at that.

4. *Go on TV.* I could totally apply to go on *School of Silence* and win loads of prizes for my class, 'cos I reckon I could not talk through anything – through people pushing my head in a cake or tickling my feet. Anything. And I'd share all the prizes with everyone in 5R, even Mr Reeve. But not Murphy. That'd show him.

And the boy decided to have a good think about which one he was going to do first. Probably one of the ones to do with cheese, if he's honest.

*The End*

Mr Reeve read my story over my shoulder and said my use of similes was excellent, and even though they didn't have red fire engines in those days – or any colour fire engines, actually – he thought it conjured up the image of someone dying a horrible death through poisoning really well.

And I'll be honest. Normally when it comes to doing anything creative, everyone always says, 'Oh, just be like your sister, 'cos she's dead dramatic.'

Always in maths, Mrs Wintour says, 'You could ask your little brother for help, what with him being in Mensa.' Imagine what it's like every time you try something to have people say one of your brothers and sisters has already done it brilliantly. Sometimes it's not even worth bothering, 'cos you're never going to do it as well as they did. So, truth be told, it felt quite nice for Mr Reeve to say something nice about my work, and not to be telling me off for mucking about like he normally does. Maybe he's not so bad after all. Maybe he should drink more lattes.

And maybe, just maybe, I might try a little bit harder with this family presentation I have to do, just like Mr Reeve says.

# Saturday 5 July

There's nothing else for it. Today I am feeling like a
Cheshire cheese. It's one of the flakiest there is.

It's pouring with rain outside, so I'm lying in bed,
flicking through a Spider-Man comic, when Jacob
barges into the room. I'm about to pick up my
notepad from the floor so I can write:

### GET OUT OF MY ROOM!!!!

Well, all right, technically it's *our* room, but still.

Then Jacob says, 'I don't know if this would be
any good?' and I realize he's got something in his
hands. It's an A3 piece of card with a diagram on it.

It looks like this:

'It's a pie chart,' Jacob explains. 'It shows that four of us have brown hair, three blond, and Susie's a redhead. I thought you could use it. For your presentation.'

I stare at him, gobsmacked.

'If you wanted to,' Jacob mumbles. 'I mean, you don't have to.'

I look over the pie chart again. I'm sure Mr Reeve would be impressed, to be fair. Then I quickly tot something up on my fingers and grab my notebook.

*FOUR* OF US HAVE BROWN HAIR??

Jacob nods. 'Yeah,' he replies. 'Ben's got brown hair.'

Just when I was starting to like him. I narrow my eyes at Jacob, as if to say, 'Why are you doing this?' There's got to be an ulterior motive. No one just helps someone without wanting anything in return.

Jacob pushes his glasses up his nose. He only got a new pair last month but maybe he needs smaller glasses 'cos they're always slipping. Or maybe he's just like Dad and his hooter's growing at an alarming rate. I really hope *that's* not a family trait. 'I'd better practise my clarinet,' is all he says.

Well, this is most unexpected. I can't really think of what else to do, so I give Jacob this little sort of smile and he beams at me and trots out of the door and down the stairs. He's not so bad, after all, I suppose.

'One day, kiddo, we'll all look back on this and laugh,' Dad says to me. 'It'll be one of those funny family stories to wheel out when you bring your first girlfriend home.'

Jacob's got his head buried in a crossword puzzle, but he scrunches up his face. 'Girlfriend,' he whispers. 'That's gross.'

Mum looks up from helping Lucy with her dinner. 'Like the time Anthony tried running away but only packed a pair of pants and a cheeseboard in his rucksack.'

'Or the time he got a piece of my Lego stuck up his nose,' Robbie says in between mouthfuls of shepherd's pie. 'Took two doctors and a shedload of tissues to get it back out.'

Everyone laughs at that and I get that image again of a zebra cowering before a pack of wild, salivating hyenas. And I'm not one of the hyenas.

'That's classic Anthony,' Susie says as she preens into her knife, using it like a mirror. 'You could write a whole book on stupid stuff he's done.'

'Isn't that what you're doing, though?' Robbie asks, nodding at my notebook. 'Writing down all your stupid stuff for your doctor? All your feeeeeel-ings?' He waggles his fingers when he says 'feelings', like it's really dumb, and Susie joins in with him.

'Oooh, feeeeeeelings,' she goes.

I have to bite down on my lip to stop from yelling at them.

'And now we've also got: remember that time Anthony went all weird and stopped talking for ages,' Robbie ploughs on, 'and nothing we could do would make him start again. Not giving him sweets, or a new Xbox game. Nothing *small*, anyway.' He looks pointedly at Mum and Dad. You can practically see him packing for California already.

I just frown at them all instead. It's definitely my best ever frowning.

Mum and Dad exchange a look. 'Come on now, that's enough,' Mum says, getting up from the table. 'You know Dr Morley says we have to let Anthony take his time. Robbie, clear the plates away, please. Susie, washing up.'

Dad shoots me a sheepish grin. 'You just keep writing, kiddo,' he says. He hoists Lucy out of her chair and takes her into the front room. Jacob trots in after them, still poring over his puzzle.

I slide up to Susie at the sink, and scribble down on my notepad:

WHAT ARE YOU PLAYING AT?

Susie looks at me blankly. 'What do you mean?'

I'M NOT TALKING SO WE CAN GO TO DISNEYLAND

'Yes?' Robbie says matter-of-factly. 'And?'

SO WHY ARE YOU STILL GOING ON ABOUT ME NOT TALKING?

Susie laughs at me playfully. 'Oh, Anthony,' she says, wiping her hands on a tea towel. 'We don't want Mum and Dad to suss we're up to something. We're just trying to act how we normally act. Right, Rob?'

Robbie nods. 'Exactly. Even though we couldn't get to Disneyland without you not talking.' He reaches over and pulls my hood up and tugs at the strings so it's pulled tightly round my face.' Susie and Robbie burst out laughing, and I can't help it – I shake my shoulders along with them. 'We need you, Ant,' Robbie says. 'But you've just got to play along with us.'

That sounds ALL RIGHT by me. THEY NEED ME!

I pick up another tea towel from the counter and the three of us work the washing-up like a factory production line. Susie starts humming away, something familiar . . .

'Hey!' Robbie goes as she begins the lyrics to 'Hall of Fame'. 'That's *my* song. Well, not *my* song, but you know what I mean.' He begins to sing along with her, and the three of us sway gently in time to the music. Susie picks up a wooden spoon and sings into it, ignoring the flecks of mashed potato around the rim.

There's a cough from the doorway, and we turn to see Mum watching us. 'Well, this is a first,' she smiles. 'Anthony, actually doing household chores.'

I give her a little bow and wave my tea towel in the air, but as Robbie and Susie laugh, a frown crosses Mum's face. 'Oh, Anthony!' she sighs. 'That's the tea towel I used to wipe Badger down this afternoon. For goodness' sake.' She storms into the kitchen and snatches the tea towel off me.

How was I meant to know? Normally the tea towel Mum uses to wipe Badger after he's been out in the rain has got claw marks on it, 'cos he hates being wiped down – he probably *wants* to get pneumonia.

'He wasn't to know,' Robbie says, springing to my defence. 'It's not his fault.'

Mum relents at that. 'I know,' she says softly. 'I'm sorry, Ant. I'm tired, that's all. Sorry.' And she waltzes back out of the kitchen.

Susie, Robbie and me all share a look, then Susie dips her hand back into the water and splashes soapy suds at the two of us. 'Don't worry about it, Ant,' she laughs. 'You know what Mum's like.'

I wipe the suds off my face and I can't help but grin back at the both of them. I suppose my family are all right, really.

Some of them. Some of the time.

## Sunday 6 July

Today I am feeling like Cambozola, 'cos it goes the best with strawberries and cream.

Today's the Men's Final at Wimbledon, so after our Sunday lunch, we all traipse into the front room to watch Andy Murray try and beat Rafael Nadal, and Dad hands us all bowls of strawberries and cream. Yummers!

And the VERY BEST thing about today? Ben's watching the match in the pub with his mates, so he's not round our house, eating our food, sitting on our sofa, bothering my family. Hooray!

While we're cheering loudly, and pumping our

fists in the air when Murray wins the first set, I add to my list:

THINGS THAT COULD BE 'MY THING'
- CIRCUS SIDESHOW ACT
- SPY & ASSASSIN
- NINJA
- POLITICIAN
- EVIL GENIUS
- TENNIS PLAYER. I don't mind wearing white. Susie owns a sweatband I could borrow. I like lemon squash. A servant hands your towel to you, you haven't got to pick it up yourself. But the VERY BEST thing? People chant your name while doing the Mexican Wave. I reckon 'Ant-o-ny! Ant-o-ny!' has a good ring to it.

It's something to think about, anyway. I am fairly sporty.

During the third set, when Murray and Nadal are sitting on their chairs, drinking their squash and each nibbling on a banana, Robbie pretends to fall over on the sofa. 'Oops,' he goes, 'I've accidentally landed on the remote. And look! It's somehow got onto this—' And he presses a button so that the YouTube channel comes up. 'Oh, what's this?' he asks all innocently, and he presses another button and an advert for Disneyland starts playing. Two kids are trying to get to sleep but they can't 'cos they're too excited about going on holiday there. 'Mum says it's simply maaaaaagical!' one kid cries, and I agree with her despite how utterly annoying she is.

'Yes, thank you, Robbie,' Dad huffs. 'You can put the tennis back on now.'

Robbie switches off the advert and puts BBC1 back on and winks at me. 'Hashtag "Just Saying",' he whispers, and I stifle a laugh.

In bed that night, I'm lying there thinking about whether Superman would beat Spider-Man in a fight and thinking he probably would, 'cos as good as Spidey is, Superman's got x-ray vision (except through lead) and laser vision so he could burn down all Spider-Man's webs just by looking at them, when I hear Jacob sigh. Blah! I hope he's not wet the bed again.

Jacob gives a big sniff. Like – he's crying. Oh God. Why's he crying? I roll over so that I'm facing him. In the darkness, I can see his eyes glistening. He looks over at me, and sniffs again.

'Sorry, Anthony,' he whispers, and his voice seems to stick in his throat. 'I didn't mean to wake you.'

There's a funny feeling in my stomach. Like – I don't know what. Something about the way Jacob's lying there looking all miserable and small makes me feel – sad. I feel sad for him. I switch on the bedside light and grab my Transformers notepad.

## WHY ARE YOU CRYING?

Jacob shakes his head. 'Doesn't matter,' he sniffs.

I thrust my notepad at him again.

## WHY ARE YOU CRYING?

Jacob wipes his eyes with the sleeve of his pyjamas. 'Space camp,' he answers, like that explains everything. He sighs and adds, 'My school are sending five pupils to NASA to observe planets during the summer holidays. It's a special programme for' – he swallows here, like he can't bring himself to say the words – 'gifted children. But they can't cover all the costs. The pupils have to get their parents to pay the rest.'

I shrug my shoulders. What's this got to do with Jacob?

Even in the semi-darkness, I can see him blush a little. 'I'm one of the five,' he says quietly.

I quickly add something to my notepad and hold it up again.

## SO – WHY ARE YOU CRYING?

Jacob props himself up on his elbows. 'Mum and Dad would never be able to afford to send me,' he says. 'It's a few hundred pounds.' He shoots me a curious look. 'Especially if we're trying to go to Disneyland.'

I frown at that. Yes, I think. We *are* trying to go to Disneyland.

In the silence, Jacob wipes his nose.

I take my notepad and write down two things.

### MAYBE NEXT YEAR, HEY?

Jacob nods. 'I guess,' he says, and he lies back down in bed. Before I switch the light off, though, I hold up my notepad once more.

### BEST NOT TELL MUM & DAD. YOU WOULDN'T WANT TO MAKE THEM FEEL BAD, WOULD YOU?

Jacob reads the note and looks at me in alarm. Before he can say anything, I switch the bedside light off and roll over in bed, my back to him.

I shut my eyes tight and put my fingers in my ears, and try and block out the sound of his sniffling.

I know saying that was mean. I know I probably should have said, 'Why don't you try Mum and Dad anyway, and see what they say. You never know – they might have a secret stash of savings somewhere.' But I didn't. 'Cos I know they haven't. They couldn't afford to send Jacob to space camp *and* the rest of us to Disneyland. Jacob can go to space camp any time. He's so clever he'll be chosen next year for sure. I'm only not talking for a little while, so I'm the one who's sorting the family holiday this year. I'm the one the rest of the Buttons are relying on.

So Jacob should stop being so selfish and just learn to live with it.

## Monday 7 July

Today I am feeling like a Pecorino Toscano cheese,
'cos it's a bit surprising.

Mr Reeve said because the new seating arrangements were going so well we're going to stick at it for a while, which means I'm now properly on Jupiter table with Jemima, Stacy and Rashid. Murphy's on Venus table with James, Stephanie and Meadow, and I didn't speak to him at all. Well, you know what I mean.

I ended up sitting next to Samir Stamford at lunch, which was a turn-up for the books. But Samir was all on his own and looking a bit sad, so

I sat down next to him, and then Rashid and Stacy came to sit with us as well, and Constance Ngoru from 5W, and we talked about *Doctor Who* and the tennis, and about Mrs Booth the music teacher's smelly breath. Well, they talked, and I did some silent laughter.

And – get this. Samir has hot dinners every day because his mum's too busy to do a packed lunch, and because the whole wide world knows that Samir's got an imaginary friend, the dinner ladies give him an extra portion of pudding. They said it was for Woody Wattler, but Samir says Woody Wattler doesn't like pudding, so he gave the spare one to me!

And – get this! It was cheesecake! And the whole wide world knows that my favourite dessert after a cheeseboard is cheesecake. He's all right, really, is Samir.

When I get home from school, Jacob's sitting at the kitchen table, whizzing through the problems in his maths book like I flick through the pages of my comics. Mum's upstairs with Lucy, and Dad's gone to town for a meeting with some client. Just as I sit down to play a bit of Xbox 'cos I've got five minutes to myself, Robbie comes waltzing into the front room.

'All right?' he goes, but he's got a plectrum stuck in the corner of his mouth, so it's more like 'Uhwwiiiite?' I nod and turn my attention back to the TV screen, but Robbie hovers in front of me. He thrusts a piece of paper at me, then takes out his plectrum. 'I've been working on something,' he says. 'You can use it if, you know, you want to. You don't have to. Whatever.'

Before I can even say anything, he flops down on the sofa next to me, picks up the Xbox controls and starts shooting away on *Halo*.

I pick up the piece of paper and it takes me a moment to work out what it's for.

This is what it says:

## FAMILY TREE

MUSIC AND LYRICS BY ROBBIE ZEPPELIN
    BUTTON

I'M LOOKING UP MY FAMILY TREE

AND WHAT IT MEANS TO ME

'COS WE ARE FAMILY

THE TREE HAS MANY LEAVES AND SHOOTS

THAT TAKE US BACK TO OUR ROOTS

WE'RE ALL DIFFERENT BUT WE'RE FROM
    THE SAME BEGINNING

WE'RE ALL DIFFERENT BUT WE'RE ALL
    WINNING.

Two things spring to mind:

1  Robbie's middle name isn't Zeppelin, he just
   calls himself that 'cos he thinks it sounds more
   rock 'n' roll.

2  Does he expect me to sing this?

All right, three things:

3. will.i.am's definitely not got anything to worry about.

'What do you think?' Robbie says after he sees me staring at it for a little while. 'I can play you the tune if you like. You don't have to use it.'

And then I feel a bit mean that I put pepper in the quiche at the picnic the other day and he accidentally ate it, 'cos he's really just trying to be nice.

The front door slams shut. 'Anthony!' Susie booms from the hallway. 'You in yet?'

She appears in the front room, a DVD in her hand. She slings her school bag down by the sofa, then settles into the armchair opposite and pulls Badger onto her lap. 'You gave him the song, then?' Robbie nods. 'I thought we could watch this,' she goes, showing me the DVD. 'It's *The Artist*. Rhiannon lent it to me. It's that silent movie, you know? To help you with miming your presentation.

It's like this.' And she jumps back up off the sofa and Badger goes flying halfway across the room and almost smacks into the mantelpiece. He looks like he enjoyed it, though. As Badger purrs for Britain and weaves himself in between Susie's legs, she places one hand in the air, palm facing outwards, then the other hand, then opens her eyes wide, looking all around her.

'What are you doing?' Robbie laughs.

'I'm trapped in a box,' Susie says.

'Why would Ant be trapped in a box?'

'It's what mime artists do. Then they act that they're pulling a heavy rope,' which she starts doing, scrunching up her face in determination and hauling on an imaginary line.

Well, I'm not being funny, but I don't fancy doing *that* in front of Year 5.

Then Jacob pops his head round the door from the kitchen. 'Would you like me to make you another chart? I could step it up to a Venn diagram.'

Whoa! All I need now is Lucy thrusting her 'touch and sing' nursery rhyme book at me to use on stage and I've got the full set. I lean over the edge of the sofa and take my notepad from my rucksack, and quickly scribble:

## WHY ARE YOU HELPING ME?

Then they all – ALL – look at me like I've just asked them, 'Why is the sky blue?' or, 'Why does xylophone start with an x?' or, 'Why *can't* you eat yellow snow?'

''Cos we *want* to help you,' Susie says matter-of-factly. 'We're family, aren't we?' Well, yes, but we've never helped each other much before. She obviously spots my confusion, 'cos she goes on, 'Look, I know how scary it is getting up in front of everyone and performing. It's not going to be easy.'

'And you're helping us get to Disneyland,' Robbie chips in, 'so it's the least we can do.'

I nod slowly as it sinks in. Then I give them a little smile and they all beam back and Susie shoves the DVD in the player and presses PLAY.

Lucy comes wandering into the front room just

then, a dummy in her mouth. 'Lucy!' Susie calls and slaps her thigh. 'Come and sit on my lap. We're going to watch a film.'

But Lucy toddles over to me – ME! – and sticks her arms in the air. So I lift her up and pull her onto my lap, 'cos clearly I'm the best brother and she only wants to cuddle *me*!

We all stay like that for a whole hour and a half while we watch these French people dance about a bit with a funny dog doing tricks every now and then.

It's a bit odd, truth be told. There's no way I'm going to be doing any of that miming malarkey in my presentation. But that doesn't mean I don't get a warm glow in my tummy 'cos I'm pleased my family are trying to help me like they've never done before.

I reckon there must be something in the water.

# Tuesday 8 July

Today I am feeling like a Pont l'Évêque.
It's a cheese that stinks so badly it makes your
smelly socks smell like roses. It's so bad that when
you smell it, you think your nose is going to fall off.
But it's all right, actually, when you eat it.

School today was all right, actually. Here's why:

1.  Mum didn't have time to pack me a lunch box this morning so I had school dinners, which was fishcake and chips with chocolate mousse for pudding.
2.  A pigeon got stuck on the roof of the library portakabin. It took Mr Farah, the caretaker,

twenty minutes to get it down, and Miss Watson kept going, 'Ooh, don't hurt it, poor thing.' Mr Reeve was laughing at Miss Watson, and she kept walloping him on the arm, going, 'Stop it!' But then when Mr Farah did get the pigeon down, Miss Watson went, 'My hero!' and Mr Reeve didn't half look mad.

3. Meadow Jenkins is the only one who's finished her presentation, but thanks to Jacob I have a pie chart for mine, which Mr Reeve said was very inventive, and he made me stand up in front of the class and show it off, which was nice. Murphy hasn't even started his yet.

4. Mr Reeve forgot to pack away his shorts after PE and Rashid found them at lunch and put them on his head and danced around and we all laughed and even Mr Reeve laughed along with us too. It was properly mint.

When Mum picks me up from school, Jacob takes Lucy straight into the front room, and I've only just kicked off my shoes in the porch when

Mum says, 'Anthony, can you come upstairs a sec?'

So I traipse upstairs behind Mum and she gestures to her bed, where there's a shoe box overflowing with photographs. 'I thought you could use these.' She motions for me to sit beside her and holds up three photos of me.

I look at her in surprise, so she says, 'For your presentation. You know, your Powerpoint.'

She looks all hopeful and everything, so I squidge next to her on the bed and take a look at the photos.

The first is of me in the bath, with a rubber duck on my head.

## THAT WILL NOT BE GOING IN THE PRESENTATION!

The second is of me trying to play football in our back garden with Robbie and Dad. I'm wearing Swindon's away kit and Robbie's in goal, and I'm trying to tackle Dad but he's grabbed me round the waist and is just about to hoist me up onto his shoulders. I guess I'm about four or five. I dunno, it's hard to tell 'cos I don't remember it.

I wish I did, 'cos it looks quite nice – me and Robbie and Dad.

The third is that flaming photo of me prancing down the stairs with a bin bag taped to my back like a cape and those flaming underpants on my head, like I'm Rashid with Mr Reeve's shorts. Maybe everyone at the presentation would laugh at that like they did in class today, but I don't want to take the chance.

Mum strokes the back of my head. 'I love that photo,' she whispers. 'It's just brilliant.'

No it's flaming not, I think. I swear this photo is haunting me.

'It's probably my favourite of all the photos I've ever taken.'

I look up at her as if to say, 'The most *ridiculous* photo, you mean?' and I see she's got a bit of a tear in her eye. 'You were adamant you wanted to go to Chessington with Robbie and his mates for his birthday, and when me and your dad said you were too young, you came waltzing down the stairs in that.' She nods at the photo. 'I just happened to have my camera on me and took it before I could burst out laughing. Honestly, Ant, it was the funniest thing.'

Mum really needs to get a new sense of humour, if she thinks *that's* funny.

'It was so sweet how much you looked up to Robbie and wanted to be like him,' Mum says. 'You used to copy his sentences and wear all his clothes, even though they were too big for you.'

Wait a minute! That's only because they were flaming hand-me-downs like most things in this family.

'I saw you with Lucy yesterday,' Mum ploughs on. 'You were the only person she wanted a cuddle from, did you notice? Lucy and Jacob look up to you, you know, just like you and Susie look up to Robbie, and Robbie looks up to Ben.'

That's only 'cos Ben's so flaming tall. Why else would anyone look up to him?

She strokes my head again. 'You're quite possibly the most stubborn person I know,' she says, and then she laughs. 'And I guess that's why you're doing so well at not talking.'

*Doing so well?* That's unexpected.

'I admire you for sticking to your guns,' Mum says, and she gazes out of the bedroom window. 'And for daring to be a bit different. I bet it's not easy not talking and sticking to it while everyone else in your class is. But, you know what, Anthony? It's the people who dare to be different in this life who go down in history.'

I'm not really sure I know what I could go down in history for. Do people who know a lot about cheese count?

'At first I didn't understand it,' Mum ploughs on. 'I got frustrated that you weren't talking. I thought it was because of something that I did wrong. But I know you and Dr Morley are working through it.'

I feel a bit mean, then, what with trying to get a holiday out of it and everything.

'I know I'm always busy with looking after everyone,' Mum says, 'and with studying and with my exams, so I'm sorry if sometimes you feel a bit left out. But it won't be for ever and I'm studying because I love it. It's something for me; I can say that I'm an accountant, as well as a mum, though that's mega-important to me too. Can you understand that?'

I guess. Mum's never had a proper job before, but I suppose now Lucy's going to nursery and we're all at school, she's probably properly bored. I nod.

'You know, Anthony,' Mum whispers, 'just because you've not found something you really enjoy yet, like Susie with her acting, or Jacob with his maths, or Robbie with his guitar – it doesn't mean you won't. It's just not your time yet, that's all.'

It's like she's read my mind in all honesty. I think in my brain, Disneyland, Disneyland, Disneyland, or at least an Xbox of my own, to see if she's really genuinely psychic or if it's a one-off.

'I know that whatever you're going to do,' she says, not mentioning holidays or computer consoles, 'you're going to be brilliant.' And she leans down and kisses the top of my head.

She looks at me all mumsily, so I take out my notepad and can't really think of what to write, except . . .

## THANKS

Then I add:

### FOR THE PHOTOS. THEY'LL COME IN HANDY.

Mum smiles, then gets up off the bed. 'You're more than welcome, my love.' She nods to the shoe box as she heads to the door. 'I'll leave you to have a look through those, see if there's any other photos you'd like, while I make a start on tea.' And she goes downstairs.

Well, that was quite nice, I think. Mum telling me that it's her favourite photo. That she admires what I'm doing. That she thinks I'm going to be brilliant at whatever I choose to do.

I'm not sure. I'm really not. Even though I keep making lists about it, and everything. But one thing *is* for sure. Whatever it is I'm going to be brilliant at, I'd really like to find out what it is, as soon as possible please.

# Tuesday 8 July

## 6.30 p.m.

If Jess wants me to put chapter headings
in this journal, this chapter would be called:

'THE ONE WHERE IT ALL KICKS OFF'

Just as Mum's called us to the table for dinner, there's a knock on the door. While Susie goes to answer it, I'm pondering what a nice couple of days I've had. School has been surprisingly OK, Mr Reeve showed me off to the class, Robbie, Susie and Jacob have helped me with my presentation and we're all being all right to each other, and Mum's told me my photo's her absolute favourite and that I might be a tiny bit brilliant, one day.

Then Dad tells this really cheesy joke – not about cheese, 'cos I think he's learned his lesson from the other day – that goes like this:

DAD: Incidentally, what lies at the bottom of the ocean, shivering?

ROBBIE: I don't know. What lies at the bottom of the ocean, shivering?

MUM: Oh God, not this one again.

JACOB: I think I know – is it the *Titanic*? 'Cos that's been down there for over a hundred years.

DAD: A nervous wreck.

Everyone groans, but I do a bit of silent laughter and Dad catches me shaking my shoulders. 'Anthony liked it,' he grins and pats me on the back.

Well, isn't this nice!

Then Susie comes back. 'Look who it is!' she trills.

And we all turn to see stupid old Ben in the doorway. 'Evening, all,' he says, and Dad gets up from the table, bobs his knees – which is no mean feat 'cos they're all old and creaky – and says, ''Ello, 'ello, 'ello,' and he and Ben burst out laughing. Hmph.

Trust them to have a secret language that no one else is allowed to know about.

Ben clears his throat. 'Mind if I have a word?'

Dad's clearly surprised, but he just says, 'Sure.'

'In private,' Ben goes. 'You too, Clare, if you don't mind.'

Well, isn't this purple beard-o?

So, while Mum, Dad and Ben sidle into the front room and talk in hushed whispers, Susie, Jacob and Robbie start pondering what on earth it's all about.

Not me, though. I couldn't care less what Ben's up to. Not me. Don't want to spend another moment of my life thinking about him.

Instead, I pick up my journal and think of the worst jokes Dad's ever told:

1. WHAT'S SANTA'S FAVOURITE PIZZA?
   One that's deep pan, crisp and even.
2. DO MOTORS HAVE EARS?
   Yes, engineers.
3. WHAT'S A SPECIMEN?
   An Italian astronaut.

4. DID YOU HEAR ABOUT THE MAN WHO BOUGHT
   A PAPER SHOP?
   It blew away.

5. WHAT DO YOU CALL A POLAR BEAR IN THE
   SAHARA DESERT?
   Lost.

'What do you reckon, Anthony?' Susie whispers across the table to me. 'What are they talking about?'

I shrug my shoulders. And then I cross my fingers 'cos I hope Ben's not mentioning his stupid football match on Thursday. Dad can't have a choice about who to watch, 'cos what if he doesn't choose me?

'Just leave him,' Robbie sighs. 'He's too busy thinking about his feelings for that book of his.'

Susie looks at me curiously. 'What *are* you writing, Ant?' she says. 'It's about us, isn't it?' And her eyes practically light up, because Susie never stops banging on about the autobiography she's going to write after she's become a world-famous actress and has been in showbiz for yonks and is all old. Like, twenty-six.

'It's bound to be about us, isn't it?' Robbie says.

'Oh, go on, Ant. Give us a look.' Susie grins. 'It'll be like getting my first review.'

I scowl at them and curl my arm round the top of the page so they can't see what I'm doing.

'It's private,' Jacob pipes up, and for the first time in a long time I feel like giving him a hug. I don't, obviously.

Mum comes bounding back into the room then, the world's biggest grin on her face. Dad and Ben follow, Dad's arm draped round Ben's shoulder.

'Are we all sitting comfortably?' Dad grins, looking down his big hooter at all of us. 'There's excellent news, Team Button. Your big brother here' – and Dad pats Ben playfully on the arm – 'has done something incredibly generous and I want you to show him how grateful we are.'

I think I'm going to be sick. That'd show him. Right over his posh, shiny shoes.

'We've revised the accounts,' Mum chips in, 'moved some money around, and now that Ben's offered to help us out we've agreed that we can afford for the Button family holiday this year – wait for it—'

'Dun, dun, dunnnnnnn,' Dad goes and Mum rolls her eyes.

'Disneyland Paris!' Ben blurts out.

WHAAAAAA?????

'OMG!' Susie gushes, leaping up from the table. She flings herself at Ben. 'Famous people go there all the time!'

Robbie nods at Dad, trying to play it cool, but I can see he's hiding a grin. 'Yeah,' he says. 'Whatever.'

'What do you say, Jacob?' Mum says, ruffling his hair. 'Excited?'

Jacob looks up at them, and for a second I think I catch a funny look in his eye. He clears his throat. 'Yeah, great,' he says. 'Thank you.'

Well, he's changed his tune, considering he kept banging on about space camp.

Mum, Dad and Ben finally turn to me and look at me with expectant faces.

'Well?' Mum says after a while. 'What do you reckon, Ant?'

I shrug my shoulders. Dad mock groans. 'Oh, come on, Ant,' he says. 'You could be a *little* more enthusiastic. It's Disneyland Paris!' And he starts dancing round the kitchen, shaking his hips and swinging his arms around. He looks like a baby giraffe stuck in tar. How's *that* for 'My Family and Other Animals'?!

I look for my notepad so that I can scribble down:

AS LONG AS YOU DON'T INSIST ON DOING *THAT* AT DISNEYLAND PARIS.

'Cos I'm not being funny, but when Dad starts dancing you want the ground to swallow you up. And then spit you out and hide you in a napkin.

But my notepad's not there and I remember that I must have left it upstairs in Mum and Dad's room when I was looking through the shoe box of photographs.

I hold up one finger as if to say, 'Hold on a second, Buttons, I shall just jog off and get my pad so I can let you know that, actually, it's not a bad plan, not a bad plan at all,' and I scrape my chair back, run out of the kitchen and up the stairs.

I dash into Mum's room, grab my notepad and trot down the stairs again. All the time I'm thinking, Hmph, I wonder what's in it for Ben? Why is he trying to buy us off like this? He'd better not be expecting to come along too, 'cos this is the BUTTON family holiday and he's not a Button – well, maybe only when he finally shuts up and BUTTONs it, ha ha ha, and I'm jumping down the stairs and thinking of a way I can introduce this into general conversation – when I realize something. I freeze mid-step.

This means I can talk now, right?

We got the holiday we all wanted – sort of – so they're all going to be expecting me to start talking again. They might even throw a parade. Fireworks, blaring trumpets, a plane writing WELL DONE, ANTHONY in letters in the sky – it's not too much to ask, is it?

I run back into the kitchen, ready to be greeted by triumphant cheers.

And everyone – EVERYONE – is stood round the table, frozen, and as I burst in, they turn to look at me.

It's deathly quiet, like someone's switched off

the mute button on the telly. Maybe they've all decided to copy my not talking so we can upgrade to Disneyland after all.

I scrabble for a fresh page in my notepad so I can write, 'What's happened? Has Mrs Taylor complained about the noise again? Did Badger finally cop it?' when Dad holds up my journal.

My journal.

He holds it open to the page where I've written: 'OPERATION GROB. Get. Rid. Of. Ben.'

'Anthony,' Dad says, and his voice is low and shaky. His eyes are wild. I've never seen him look like this before. He grits his teeth and says, very slowly, 'What. Is. This?'

And in his other hand he holds up the photograph Ben gave me of him as a boy.

The one I've scribbled on.

The one where I've written: MY NAME IS BEN AND I'M A LOOOOOOOOOOOOOSER, and I HAVEN'T GOT A REAL FAMILY OF MY OWN SO THAT'S WHY I HAVE TO GO ROUND STEALING OTHER PEOPLE'S.

Oh. Flaming. Heck.

Mum looks at me with tears in her eyes. 'How could you?' she says, and she looks like she's just heard I've done a murder. Ben's shaking his head at me, while Susie and Robbie keep exchanging looks like they know it's going to kick off at any moment. Only Jacob's not looking at me, and just stares at the table. You could cut the tension with a cheese wire.

I gulp. My ears feel all hot. Now would be a good time, a really good time for the ground to open up. For the ground to swallow me whole and never, ever burp me back up again.

'Would you care to explain yourself?' Dad says, and I can see the anger flash in his eyes. His eyebrows are so tightly woven into a frown they're in danger of slipping down his face and becoming a moustache. 'Anthony,' he adds in a voice so low it's practically a growl. 'You'd better start talking.'

I shrink back a bit, just as Mum grabs Dad's arm and steadies him. 'Phil,' she murmurs, and then looks over at me, 'cos she's seen the panic on my face. 'Anthony,' she says softly. 'Please.

Just what were you thinking? Come on, love. Talk to us.'

'This ends now,' Dad says.

Mum rubs his arm. 'You know what Dr Morley said.'

Dad shakes her off. 'I don't give two hoots what she said. I want to know what Anthony thinks he's playing at, defacing this photo, writing awful stuff about his own brother, and I want to know *now*.'

Even Susie and Robbie shrink back at that. They look at me like they know I'm about to be bundled off before the firing squad. Everyone's standing round waiting for an answer, and Dad looks like he's about to have a heart attack.

'Your own brother!' Dad yells.

'HE'S NOT MY BROTHER!!'

For a split second, I wonder where that came from, but then I realize it was me. *I* blurted it out. It sounded all cracked, 'cos I've not spoken in so long. My throat feels dry.

I didn't think Dad's face could look any more

shocked, but his jaw drops so low it's in danger of breaking free. 'WHAT?' he thunders.

I gulp again. I mean, I hadn't meant for that to come out. Even though it's true.

'What did you say?' Dad repeats.

And that's it! No, 'Oh my gosh, Anthony's started talking again! Please can we just all appreciate this momentous occasion? Maybe a round of applause for my son?' Certainly no fireworks and skywriting.

I shrug my shoulders. 'He's not my brother,' I croak. 'Not really. So I don't know why everyone's so upset.'

Dad inhales sharply. Then he walks over to Ben and places a reassuring hand on his shoulder. 'I'm so sorry,' Dad says softly.

'Why are you apologizing to *him*?' I say. 'All right, I shouldn't have scribbled on his stupid photo, but I didn't want it in the first place. He just forced it on me. I didn't *ask* for it.'

'That's enough,' Dad says. He shakes his head. 'In all my life, Anthony, I never thought you could be this selfish. Go to your room.'

I fold my arms. 'It's my personal diary!' I shout. 'You had no right reading it!'

Dad takes a deep breath. 'Ben's gone out of his way to try and be a part of this family, and you throw it back in his face!'

'I didn't ask him to!'

'GO TO YOUR ROOM!' Dad booms. 'I don't want to hear another peep out of you, do you understand?'

I narrow my eyes at him. 'Do you want me to answer, 'cos I thought you didn't want to hear another peep?'

'Anthony,' Mum says. 'Please, just, go upstairs.'

I stamp my foot. 'Fine!' I shout at all of them. 'I hate you. I hate you all!'

And with that I run out of the kitchen and pound upstairs, the sound of my feet stomping on the carpet matching the rushing, thumping sound in my ears.

I SLAM the door of my room shut so hard that it wobbles a bit and the chest of drawers under the window rattles. 'Nobody even cares that I'm talking again!' I shout to the door, loudly so that I know they'll still be able to hear me in the kitchen. 'All this time, and I'm talking again! Well, SHOUTING! And nobody cares! Nobody cares about me!'

I storm over to the chest of drawers, and from the cardboard box Ben plonked there the other day I lift out his stupid wheel of cheese. It's a Cheddar, which is just about the most boring you can get. I throw the cheese down on the chest of drawers, pretending it's Ben's head. THUMP! And then I take the cheese knife from the cardboard box and plunge it right into the middle of the wheel of cheese.

It doesn't make me feel any better.

I fling myself down on the bed and cover my eyes with my arm, trying to block out the voices of my family drifting upstairs. This is just horrible. Nobody cares about *my* feelings. Never mind that they read my diary, which is totally rude and practically against the law. Nobody cares that I don't want Ben as a brother. Nobody cares that I've started talking again.

It's all been about stupid old Ben. LIKE ALWAYS.

# Wednesday 9 July

Today I am feeling like a Casu Marzu. It's the worst kind of cheese. It's got maggots living in it, and it's only safe to eat if the maggots are STILL ALIVE!!! They don't even sell it in shops, or let it be entered into cheese competitions or anything 'cos it's so bad. You'd only ever eat it if you were desperate and had nothing else to eat and you wanted to kill yourself.

Nobody's talking at breakfast, like they're all trying to give me a taste of my own medicine. When I say, 'Can you pass me the sugar please, Susie?' instead of her saying, 'Of course, Anthony, my favourite brother. Remember how I gave you that hairband and said we were bound to each other now? Is there anything else I can do for you? Polish your shoes?

Pour you some more juice?' she just scowls and shoves the sugar bowl at me so hard that half the bowl spills onto the table.

Mum's wiping down the kitchen counter, her back to me so she hasn't got to talk to me. 'Jacob get off to school all right, Mum?' I ask her between mouthfuls of Rice Krispies.

Mum nods her head but doesn't turn round. My own mum, not talking to me!

Robbie shoots me a look like I'm the mould that's growing in the corner of his converted-garage-bedroom, gets up from the table and flicks my ear.

'Owww!' I clamp my hand to the side of my head, but no one says anything.

Then Dad appears in the doorway, rattling the car keys. 'Right, you lot,' he says, and even though I'm staring at him he only looks at Mum, Susie and Robbie and never at me the whole time. 'School.'

Mum hands me my lunch box and gives me a tight little smile.

That's it. One little smile. No words.

Nothing.

School's not much more brilliant. Even though Mum gave me that little smile, I know she's properly angry with me 'cos she only put one measly cheese string in my lunch box – no Brie, no Gorgonzola, no Manchego.

I couldn't be bothered to talk in class. Mr Reeve didn't ask me any questions about the poem from the First World War we were meant to be looking at, and Stacy, Rashid and Jemima on my table just left me alone, so I carried on not talking. People seem to like me more when I'm not talking.

What's annoying about only having one poxy old cheese string is that I'd been looking forward to lunch all day.

I get into the dining hall and spot Murphy and Michael Hadley carrying their lunch trays to a table.

On the other side of the hall, Samir's sitting at a table on his own, so I head over and slump in the seat next to him.

'YOU'RE SITTING ON WOODY WATT-LER!!!' Samir yells at me, and I jump up like I've sat on a bee – again – while the WHOLE SCHOOL turns to look.

A drop of sweat trickles down my back. EVERYONE'S LOOKING AT ME! At the teachers' table, Mr Reeve looks over from where he's deep in conversation with Miss Watson, and 'cos he's looked away from her for a few seconds Miss Watson's turned to talk to Mr Farah and Mr Reeve's face goes all mad and thundery and he looks like he's going to throttle me.

Well, he'd better get in line.

I open my mouth, about to stutter 'Sorry,' when Samir throws his head back and laughs like a loony bin. His mouth's open so wide, I can see his tonsils.

'Only joking,' Samir says, wiping tears from his eyes. 'Woody Wattler's right here.' He points to the empty space on the other side of him.

At the table in the corner of the hall, Murphy huddles in to Michael Hadley and laughs, looking at me the whole time. Then he clears his throat, and coughs really loudly. 'MUTANT!' Michael Hadley can't help himself, and sniggers. Murphy coughs again. 'MUTANT TABLE!' he half coughs, half shouts, and the rest of the school still look over at me and Samir. Geez, Murphy could at least be *original*.

I slouch down in my seat. I find a spot on the table that looks absolutely fascinating and stare at it for what feels like seventeen hours.

As the rest of the school eventually turn back to their lunches, Samir leans in to me. 'You're not mad, are you?' he whispers, suddenly looking all serious. 'It was just a joke.'

I shrug my shoulders and bite off the top of my cheese string, imagining I'm a raven biting off the top of Samir Stamford's wormy head.

Samir chatters away to Woody Wattler about some nonsense or other and I'm still staring down at the spot on the table, thinking how utterly rubbish my life is.

I sense someone hovering behind me.

'All – all – all – all right?' a voice stutters.

I spin round to see Frankie Mellor looking down at us, a clipboard clutched in her arms.

Samir gestures to the table. 'Frankie!' he booms. 'Would you like to join us?'

She shakes her head so that strands of hair cover her face and her eyes just about peek out from under her fringe. 'I ju-ju-ju—' she starts. She takes a deep breath. 'I ju-just wanted t-t-t-to say,' she ploughs on, all the while her cheeks turning a bit pink. After a moment, she rolls her eyes, then pulls off a sheet of paper from her clipboard and hands it to me.

It says:

I can't understand why you don't talk. How you can choose not to. I'd give anything to be able to speak freely, but I can't 'cos of this stupid impediment of mine. Do you know what it feels like? It feels like every time I go to say something, there's this invisible force clamping my mouth shut, and inside

my head I'm screaming. I'm screaming
because I can't get the words out. I
hate talking in public because I know
I'm going to stammer every single time,
and if I had the gift of being able to
talk how and when I wanted, I wouldn't
waste it on being stupid.

Where's all this coming from?

I turn the piece of paper over and take my pen
from my trouser pocket.

## IT'S NONE OF YOUR BUSINESS

I write.

Frankie sighs. 'I–I'm s-s-sorry everyone l–laughed
at you ju-ju-ju-ju-just then,' she says, 'b-but it's
your ch-choice.' And with that, she holds up
the clipboard so that it's a sort of shield, covering
her face from the rest of the dinner hall, and
scuttles off.

I turn to Samir to see if he's as confused and

outraged as me, but instead, he gulps. 'She's sort of right, you know,' he says. Sheesh! Here I was, thinking he was a friend – well, sort of friend – and he's just completely stabbed me in the back. Like he's got so many pals he can afford to annoy me! 'It is your choice you're not talking,' Samir ploughs on. 'And I guess it's annoying for Frankie to see you at Dr Morley's, when she's got a real problem.'

I narrow my eyes at him but he doesn't really notice, 'cos he's looking at the empty space where Woody Wattler is standing.

'At first getting four lots of stuff was really fun,' he says, and even though he's looking at Woody Wattler, I know he's really talking to me. 'Four Xboxes, four Teenage Mutant Ninja Turtles bean bags,' he continues. 'Mum got me two lots of stuff so that Woody Wattler wouldn't be left out, then Dad did the same so that when I visit him it's just like being at home. But it's a bit rubbish having to live in one house half the week, then live in the other the rest. I'd rather both Mum and Dad were still together, but Mum says, "That's life."' Samir looks back at me, and his eyes are watery. He takes a big sniff. 'Dr Morley says I created Woody Wattler to help me get through a tough time. Mum and Dad's divorce. 'Cos I didn't really have anyone else I could talk to. I know he's not real, you know. I know the other kids laugh at me and call me stupid names. But I don't care. So, yeah. Like Frankie says. You're lucky. And you're stupid for not talking.'

I frown at him, then make a note at the bottom of the piece of paper.

## LUCKY???

Samir sighs. 'I'd give anything to be like you. To have brothers and sisters and a mum and dad that get on and love each other and love you and stuff. I'd love a shambolic family like yours. So, yeah. Lucky.'

What on earth is going on today? What is everyone's problem?

Before I can even say anything to him, before I can even write down, 'Samir Stamford, you purple beard-o, you don't even know what you're talking about. You know nothing about my family and how horrible they are to me sometimes. You know nothing about stupid old Ben swanning into my life and taking Mum and Dad's love away from me. You know nothing about what it's like having brothers and sisters who are brilliant at stuff, while you're just rubbish and all you do is like cheese,' Samir sighs, leaps up from the table and saunters off across the dining hall.

# Wednesday 9 July

## 4.10 p.m.

When I get home that afternoon, I really wish I'd invited Samir round so he could see for himself how horrible my family are.

Mum picks me up from school and she's chatting away to Jacob about his maths homework and his clarinet practice and then she puts the radio on and starts singing along to Beyoncé. She doesn't even talk to me again. I mean, all right, she asked me, 'What do you fancy for tea?' and, 'How's the presentation coming along?' but I was so annoyed she wasn't talking to me I didn't answer her.

Then when we get home Robbie's already there,

in the garage, practising his guitar with Smithy and Mark, and he only comes into the kitchen once, to get some bottles of Coke and packets of crisps, and he just nods at me. And Susie's upstairs in her room reading *Romeo and Juliet* and she doesn't even bother shouting, 'Hello' to me when I get in.

But this is the worst. 'Cos after a little bit of watching *Horrible Histories* on TV, I can hear Dad in his office, tapping away on his computer and making the 'Hmph' and 'Ooh' noises to himself, like he always does when he's deep in thought. I can hear him pacing about too, which is what he does when he's stuck on a problem. As I'm about to get up and knock on his office door to see if he's still mad at me, Mum stops me and says, 'Just leave your dad to it, Ant. He's on a tight deadline, so he'll be up working all night.'

But I reckon it's a lie. I reckon he's just trying to avoid me; to avoid looking at me, like he did at breakfast this morning.

So instead I head straight upstairs and I get into bed, and I don't even care that I'm still in my school uniform. I pull the duvet right up over my head and squeeze my eyes shut.

Mum comes up a bit later to tell me dinner's ready, but I just ignore her, and squeeze my eyes shut tighter. I'm not hungry anyway. After a few minutes, Mum sighs and shuts my door.

I guess I must have fallen asleep for real, because when I open my eyes again it's pitch dark and moonlight is streaming through a break in the curtains. I can hear Jacob's soft breathing in the next bed. I climb from under the duvet and change into my pyjamas and, seeing as I'm up, figure I'd better go to the loo.

There's a chink of light coming through the gap at the bottom of Susie's bedroom door, and as I cross the landing she whips the door open.

'Anthony!' she calls to me softly, looking up from the desk where she's straining to read Selena Gomez's autobiography by the light of the desk lamp. She's not allowed to put the main light on, 'cos she shares a room with Lucy, and Lucy'll wake up if there's too much noise or light. That's what you get for living in a three-bedroomed house with a converted garage. 'You got a minute?'

I pad over to her room and sit myself down on her bed.

'Are you not talking again?' she asks.

I stick out my bottom lip a bit as if to say, 'Whatever.'

Susie frowns. 'I'll take that as a yes, then.' She flips her hair back. 'Why can't you just tell us what's wrong? It's obvious you're annoyed that Ben's just shown up out of nowhere.' My notepad's in my bedroom, safely tucked away with my journal under my pillow so that no one else can read it, but even before I can think about getting up to fetch it Susie says, 'I get it, Ant. He's someone else in this family to think about, and our family's big enough as it is. Right?' She narrows her eyes and looks into mine, and it's like she's looking into my very soul.

I gulp.

'Ben turning up out of the blue has been a huge shock to everyone,' Susie continues, like she's acting in some TV drama. I bet she's rehearsed this little speech too. 'But it's happened now, so we've all just got to live with it. You're the only one who's not even tried to get on with Ben. How do you think that makes Ben feel? Not very welcome, I bet. How do you think that makes *Dad* feel? He's a good dad, isn't he? So he just wants to make up to Ben for all the time he's missed out being with him 'cos he didn't know he existed, and there you are being all moody and attention-seeking the whole time.'

I stand up 'cos I don't have to listen to this. What does *she* know? I storm across the room to the door, but Susie grabs my arm.

'Ant,' she pleads, keeping her voice low so as not to disturb Lucy. 'Do you not think it's annoying or hurtful when people joke about *me* being the odd one out 'cos I've got red hair and no one else does? Do you not think that makes me feel like an outsider in my own family?'

I look at her and see that she's got tears in her eyes. And this time, I don't even think she's acting. I shrug her hand off my arm, though, and slope out of the door. I mean, honestly.

I traipse back to my room and the smell of wee hits me as soon as I walk in the door. For goodness' sake! Jacob is standing by the open window, gazing up at the night sky. *That's* not going to change the sheets, is it?

'S-sorry, Ant,' Jacob sniffs. 'I – I didn't mean to.'

That's what he always says.

I climb back into bed and close my eyes, when Jacob clears his throat. 'At last count,' he says softly, 'it's estimated there are two hundred billion stars in the Milky Way.'

I don't say anything to that, 'cos I can tell he's about to go off on one of his little brainy fact-filled sessions and I'm not in the mood.

'Two hundred billion,' Jacob repeats, unfazed by my lack of interest. 'Imagine that!'

Eyes still shut, I reach under my pillow and feel for my notebook. I can tell I'm going to have to point at the 'GO AND SIT IN THE AIRING CUPBOARD' page again.

'Makes us feel insignificant,' Jacob mumbles. 'And,' he adds, 'did you know some rats can have up to twenty-four babies in one litter.'

No, I think, I didn't know. What's that got to do with anything?

'Twenty-four! Think of the food bills!' And he laughs like it's the funniest thing. Jacob's not very good at telling jokes, and for him that was comic gold. This is what I have to put up with.

I open my eyes and flick through my notepad.

I find the 'GO AND SIT IN THE AIRING CUPBOARD' page, and just as I'm about to show it to him, Jacob says, 'So, I know *we've* got a large family, but it could be worse.'

How? How could it be worse than having four really talented siblings, even though one of them is only two, and one new imposter?

Jacob clears his throat again. 'But sometimes,' he says, and his voice is barely above a whisper, 'sometimes I feel that I don't belong. Not properly. That maybe I got swapped at birth or something.'

Well, that's odd. How can Jacob not feel like he belongs to this family when he's the flaming super-smart star of it?

'I didn't ask to be sent to a special school,' Jacob mutters. 'I didn't ask to be different. I know you all think I'm geeky and brainy and weird.'

He looks at me with such ... *sadness* ... that I actually feel a bit sorry for him. So I place the notepad back under my pillow and squeeze my eyes shut again so that I haven't got to look at his sad, pitying, annoying little face any more.

I wake again a little while later. The alarm clock on Jacob's bedside table reads 02:08. In the darkness I can make out Jacob's little form on the floor by the side of his bed. I'm sleepy, but my mind's whirring with all sorts of thoughts so that every time I close my eyes it feels like my brain might explode. I can't stop thinking about what Samir said this afternoon. About how he'd love to have my family. And then I think about what Jacob said, and about what Susie said. That sometimes, just sometimes, they feel like outsiders in this family too. I'm not the only one who feels like that. I guess it's like Jess's quote on the wall of her office:

*Imagine what it might be like to be someone else.*

My eyes fall on the stupid wheel of cheese Ben bought me, and the cheese knife that's sticking straight up out of it. I throw back the duvet and clamber out of bed. I pull the knife out of the cheese so that a little bit of the Cheddar crumbles away, and shove it in my mouth, 'cos I'm starving after missing dinner, and eating cheese always makes me feel better and never gives me nightmares.

The moonlight's shining through the curtains, creating shadows on the wheel of cheese, but the bit that I've just cut out looks a little like a door. Ha! I take the knife and cut out another block. That's a window. And another. And another. And before I know it, I've chipped away enough cheese from the wheel so that it's starting to look like a house. *Our* house, with the converted garage next door.

Beside his bed, Jacob stirs softly. He lets out a little sigh. Another thought pops into my head. I place the knife beside the wheel of cheese, then creep to the bedroom door and shuffle round it onto the landing. I open the airing-cupboard door and squeeze inside.

I have to squat a bit, 'cos there's a shelf at the top of the cupboard where Mum keeps the towels and bed sheets, and my nose is right next to the boiler, which is toasty warm but it's old and creaks and bangs and I can hear water gurgling through the pipes.

And all of a sudden, there's a pang in my chest and my stomach churns like there's cement in it, and it makes the same sound as the boiler's pipes. I chew the inside of my cheek, 'cos I don't think that feeling in my stomach is from the cheese. I think it's 'cos I'm thinking of all the times I've made Jacob come and sit in here.

That was a bit harsh, I think to myself. Just 'cos Jacob was trying to start a conversation with me, or say something he thought was funny, or tell me a bit about his day at school. 'Cos thinking about it, it's not very nice in here at all, truth be told.

I duck out from under the shelf and reach up and take out a set of Jacob's bedding. Back in our room, I take off the sodden, wee-stained sheets and replace them with fresh, clean ones. I screw the old ones up in a ball and shove them in the laundry basket and then I nudge Jacob with my foot. He rubs his eyes as he wakes and I point to his bed. He takes a moment to work out what I've done, and then looks at me in amazement. 'Don't make a song and dance about it,' I whisper and climb back into my bed before he can say anything.

It's the least I could do, I suppose.

# Thursday 10 July

Today I am feeling like a Cornish Yarg cheese. I ate it once and it didn't agree with me, and my stomach was in knots for the whole day afterwards. Just like now.

Mr Reeve said 'Well done' to me today, which was nice, because I'm feeling all nervous about the presentation.

IT'S THE PRESENTATION TODAY!

Like I haven't got a million other things to be worrying about.

When Mr Reeve said at morning registration he was very much looking forward to all our presentations and how creative and different he knows we're going to make them, no one said anything and I could tell by the look on everyone's face that they were all as terrified as me. So I flipped open my notepad and wrote:

I FEEL LIKE WE'RE GETTING READY TO
GO OVER THE TOP.

Which is what they did in the First World War when they had to go over the top of the trenches and into no man's land to fight the Germans, and most of them didn't make it through without being blown up or shot or stepping on a bomb. Mr Reeve looked pleased as punch that I'd been paying attention in class and he beamed at me and said, 'That's the spirit,' which is a bit off.

After numeracy hour, I get called to the office to go to another session with Jess, and as I'm walking down the corridor to reception, I'm wondering whether it's Mum or Dad who's got the honour of taking me.

It's neither.

Sitting squashed onto a plastic chair under the office window, his knees practically under his chin, is Ben.

Flaming Nora.

My stomach flips over a bit and I wonder if I've got time to turn round and run off again—

Too late. He's seen me.

Ben gets up from the chair and sort of unfolds his limbs. 'All right, Anthony?' he says, like it's the most natural thing in the world that he's here. 'Your mum had some sort of crisis with Lucy and Dad's got a deadline, so you're stuck with me, I'm afraid.' He stands there, towering over me, smiling goofily down his big conk of a nose. 'I'll take you out for ice cream after, if you like.' Like he can just buy me off.

In the car on the way to the psychology practice, Ben switches on Radio 1 and some rubbish song by The Saturdays blasts out. He keeps clearing his throat, and after about twenty-seven hours, he starts to speak. And it's all rubbish. He's so boring I'd rather listen to The Saturdays, which just shows how desperate I am. This is what's going through my mind:

BORING BORING BORING BORING BORING BORING BORING BORING BORING BLAH BLAH BLAH BLAH BLAH BLAH BLAH BLAH BLAH BLAH BLAH BLAH BLAH BLAH BLAH I BET I COULD TOTALLY BE THE DOCTOR. THEN I'D SONIC SCREWDRIVER BEN OUT OF OUR LIVES BLAH BLAH BLAH BLAH BLAH BLAH BORING BORING BORING BORING BORING BORING BORING BORING BORING BORING HE'D FLAMING WELL BETTER GET ME A FLAKE WITH MY ICE CREAM BORING BORING BORING BORING BORING BORING BORING BLAH STOP GOING ON ABOUT HUNTER & SONS! BLAH BLAH BLAH BLAH BLAH.

When we eventually get to Jess's, it doesn't take me long to figure out that Dad's obviously had a word with her. Not least 'cos the first thing she says when she opens the door to her office is, 'Ah, this must be Ben. Your dad told me he was bringing you here.'

Ben stands behind me, and his face turns bright red and he goes to say, 'Yes,' but instead this embarrassing sort of squeak comes out and I burst out laughing. Ben stares at the ground and I can tell he's wishing it would open up and swallow him whole.

Jess gives him a polite smile, then holds the door open wider for me. 'Come on in then, Anthony,' she says and Ben shuffles off to reception and starts messing around on his iPhone.

Jess settles down beside her desk and I take my place in the chair opposite her. After a few moments, she says, 'Anything interesting happen the past couple of days?' and I can just tell it's a trick question, especially now I know Dad's phoned her. I bet he's told her everything. I bet he's made it sound like it's all my fault. Just like I bet that Ben's only pretending to be nice to me and bring me here but he's probably plotting to murder me on the way home. His very own OPERATION GET RID OF ANTHONY. Like heck we're going out for ice cream.

I shrug.

'Anything in your journal you'd like to show me?' she asks.

Not really, no.

Jess leans forward in her seat. 'Your dad also mentioned what happened the other night.'

I shrug my shoulders again, but Jess says, 'About him reading your journal. That must have been annoying, huh?'

I nod.

'Progress!' Jess laughs. 'You know, Anthony, I think this could be a really good opportunity to tell me how you're feeling. From the sound of it, you've had an up-and-down couple of days. I think it would help.' I let out a sigh and Jess laughs again. 'You see! That's the first noise you've made here.'

'I laughed just now,' I say, before I realize what I'm doing. It sort of just squeaked out, that, like Ben's 'Yes' squeaked out, but my squeak was because I've not talked for so long and my vocal cords are all rusty and cobwebby, probably.

'Ha!' Jess smiles at me. 'Yes, you did. At your brother.'

'He's not my brother,' I mumble.

'Well, then. Let's talk about that.'

I know Jess isn't trying to pull a trick on me by making me talk. And maybe she has got a point. I look down at my school shoes. One of my shoelaces is all frayed at the end. Must remember to get Mum to sort that out.

'Anthony?'

I clear my throat. Right. Yes. Here goes.

'Dad's acting like he's known Ben all his life when he's known *us* all his life, and he's not spending half as much time with us as he is with Ben,' I say.

And that's it! I'm off! Now I've started talking it feels really good, and I can't believe I've actually managed to stop talking for so long.

'Dad's busy enough as is it, what with work and keeping up with Swindon,' I plough on, 'and Mum's always stressed trying to cook or sort Lucy out or study, so when Ben comes round ours for dinner, or joins us in the park, or dares to come into my room, even if Jacob's in there, it means there's less time for Mum and Dad to be spending with the rest of us. With me.'

Jess nods at me encouragingly.

'And now Ben's really good at football, which means that I can't be.'

'Why not?'

I swing my feet under the chair. 'Just 'cos.'

'Just 'cos what?'

I let out a huge sigh. I've come this far, I may as well tell her the whole truth. ''Cos if Ben's good at football, there's no point me even trying to be good at it 'cos I'll never be as good as him. Like I'll never be as good as Robbie at the guitar, or Jacob at maths, or Susie at acting, so what's the point?'

Jess studies my face for a moment or two. I'd love to know what she's thinking. It's probably:

WHAT SHALL I HAVE FOR TEA?

DID I LEAVE THE IRON ON?

WHO IS THIS PURPLE BEARD-O SAT IN FRONT OF ME?

## HIS SHOELACE NEEDS REPLACING.

'So why don't you tell me what you *are* good at?' Jess says eventually.

I huff at this, 'cos I don't know how many times I can keep telling people it doesn't matter that I'm good at cheese. Who's ever cared about anyone who's good at cheese??

'Let's look at the evidence,' Jess ploughs on. 'You're good at not talking.'

I shrug at that. 'Anyone could do that. I'm nothing special.'

'I beg to differ. How long was it before the rest of your classmates started talking again when they tried to get out of their presentation?'

My mouth forms a perfect 'o'. 'How do you know about that?'

'Your teacher, Mr Reeve,' Jess explains. 'I've been in touch with him about you once or twice.'

Sheesh kebab! Oh God, I hope he didn't tell her about the bogey banana!

'So, you see,' Jess says, 'you're pretty special when it comes to stamina and willpower. What about thinking of something that would put those skills to use?'

'I thought everyone *wanted* me to stop not talking?' I say, confused.

Jess laughs. 'Think about *other* activities that might use those skills.'

The clock on the wall ticks slowly as I think and think and think a bit more.

After a moment or two, when it's become pretty clear that I'm rubbish at thinking too and there's probably nothing that I'm ever going to be any good at, despite what Mum said to me the other day, Jess says, 'Did I ever tell you about the time I ran the London Marathon?'

I shake my head. If she bangs on for another few minutes, I'll have more time to think.

'Three years ago,' she trills. 'Raised about two thousand pounds. I had a little bib tacked on my T-shirt, with my name on the front and the NSPCC logo on the back. In the end it took four hours and forty-seven minutes to run it, but I did it. Crossing that finish line was the best moment of my life. 'Cos somewhere along the way, around mile twenty, I think, all I wanted to do was give up. I'd been running for hours, my feet were sore, I could feel blisters on my toes; I just didn't think I could go on.'

She gazes at me like Dad does when he wants me to know that what he's about to say is an Important Life Lesson, like, 'Always look left AND right before crossing the road,' or, 'Don't talk to strangers,' or, 'Don't drink milk when it's off, Anthony, it's not cheese. Anthony, stop drinking it! Anthony! Put it down, for heaven's sake!'

'And then I heard my name being shouted,' Jess continues. 'I'd slowed down practically to a walk, struggling to get my breath, clearly in pain, when this old woman I'd never met before starts shouting, "Come on, Jess, you can do it!" It's only because she's seen my name on the front of my bib, but somehow it gives me the strength to keep going. And I do. I put one foot in front of the other and I carry on, slowly but surely, all the way to the blessed finish. And it was such a feeling of relief and pride and amazement that I'd done it.' She looks at me expectantly.

'Do you want me to run a marathon?' I ask eventually. 'Or shout at people who do?'

Jess laughs at that. 'All I'm saying is, long-distance running is just one example of the sort of thing you need stamina and willpower for.'

'I don't know . . .' I say hesitantly. I've never really thought about running before. 'I did quite like carving cheese last night.'

'Well, there you go,' Jess replies. 'That requires patience and stamina – think of all the hours of work that go into carving those massive statues made out of cheese, or butter.' She positively beams at me. 'The point is, Ant, you can be anything you want to be. It doesn't matter whether your brothers and sisters are or aren't doing it too. You've just got to work out what your thing is – what the thing you love doing the most is – and work hard at it. Stamina, patience, willpower. You've got it all in spades. You, my boy, could do anything.'

She's starting to sound a bit like Mr Reeve now.

'Dare to dream, 5R!' Or The Script. I can just imagine her breaking into 'You can be a champion!'

'And your family will love you all the same whatever,' she adds.

I'm not sure about that, but I can't help it, and I smile right back at her.

Jess stands up and heads to the door. As I get up off the chair and walk towards her, she leans down and gives me a great big bear hug.

'What's that for?' I say, but it comes out all muffled 'cos my face is pressed into her armpit.

Jess disentangles herself from me, and beams at both me and Ben as he hovers in the doorway. 'I've just got a feeling this is the last time I'll see you,' she says.

Well, that's pretty mysterious. Oh, heck, maybe *she* thinks Ben's going to murder me as well. OPERATION GET RID OF ANTHONY is very much a GO.

Jess and Ben shake hands and then we CLACK CLACK our way across reception. I turn to look back at Jess and she gives me a little wave, and a nod and a smile, as if to say, 'You just have a little ponder on what I've said, Anthony my boy, and you'll be all right, you will.'

Grown-ups are strange.

I'll say this for Ben. He didn't murder me. Or put pepper in my ice cream. Which is something, I suppose.

And, if I'm being completely honest, I probably couldn't blame him for wanting to, what with me scribbling all over his baby photo and everything. I wonder if he's told his mum. If *my mum* found out anyone had scribbled over that photo of me with a bin bag taped to my back, they'd cop it for sure.

After we leave Jess's office, Ben drives us to the park and he goes for vanilla ice cream 'cos he's boring like that, while I have two scoops of chocolate and toffee fudge. I sit down at a picnic table and watch as Ben pays the man and carries the ice creams over to me, trying not to drop them as the ice cream's running all down his fingers.

Ben hands me my ice cream, sits down opposite

me and licks the ice cream off his hands. 'Glad you find it funny,' he laughs. I don't say anything, 'cos it's not *that* hilarious. 'Everything all right with your doctor?' he asks, chomping away on his flake.

I think for a moment and say, 'You fancy her, don't you?'

Ben splutters on his ice cream. 'Yeah,' he agrees eventually. 'She's fit.' He's looking at me in shock, like I'm an alien that's landed from outer space and I've demanded to speak to his leader, 'cos obviously *Ben's* not the leader of the human race. Not with that conk. 'That's the first thing you've ever said to me,' he says after a moment. 'Well, apart from the "I like cheese" comment the first time I met you. And then the other night's "He's not my brother". Though that wasn't really *to* me, I suppose.'

I shrug my shoulders like 'whatever', and Ben takes a deep breath. He puts his ice cream down on a napkin on the bench, even though he's still got half the cone to finish.

'You know, Anthony,' he says, 'the last few weeks have been really tough, what with finding Dad and everything.' He stares around at the other people in the park; there's a mum pushing her baby in a buggy around the track while doing lunges at the same time. An old man's walking a little Yorkshire terrier who keeps yapping at the birds. Ben sighs. 'I – I've never been as nervous in my whole life as I was when I met you all in Pizza Express. And I couldn't believe it when we all got on.' He looks directly at me. 'But I just couldn't work out what I'd done wrong when you didn't speak to me. Apart from me being born, of course.'

I don't say anything to that, 'cos he's pretty much spot on.

'All I wanted was for Dad – for all of you – to like me. To fit in. I've – I've never had a family before, a proper family like you. It's just been me and my mum all these years,' he goes on. 'I'd dream about having a family. All the nights I used to lie awake thinking about who my dad was and what had happened to him. Half the reason I like bands like The Maccabees and Kings of Leon is 'cos they're bands made up of families. I used to think that could be me.'

I shoot him this look, like, 'There's NO WAY I'm being in a band with you, pal. Robbie and Susie might, but I wouldn't even play the *triangle* with you.'

Ben doesn't catch my frown and bangs on, 'I see you all with your *Oh, Dad's jokes are so naff, what does he know about anything? Look at the embarrassing dad dancing*, but I've never had that. I'm not in on the in-jokes. And I want to be. So, yeah, once I'd met you all, I just wanted to see all of you all the time, 'cos I think you're all ace.'

The old man puts his dog back on the lead and stuffs a carrier bag in the 'dog poo' bin.

'I understand why you said those things about me in your journal,' Ben says. 'And why you defaced my photo. I'm not cross – I get it. I get that it's hard for everyone, me showing up out of nowhere. But I honestly don't want to tread on any toes. I'm not trying to worm my way into the family or anything,' he says. 'I'm not trying to take Dad away from you all. I just like *having* a dad now, after all this time.' He takes a deep breath. 'You didn't tell Dad

about my match, did you?' he says, his voice barely
a whisper.

I shake my head.

Ben lets out a puff of air. 'Never mind, it's not too
late. I still might.'

'Don't,' I blurt out, before I really know what I'm
doing. 'Don't tell him.'

Ben's eyebrows shoot up in surprise.

'I – I . . .' I struggle to find the words. 'It's the
same time as my presentation, your match,' I stutter,
'and he'll choose to watch you and not me. He'll
choose you, I know he will. They all hate me 'cos
of what I did and what I said, so they'll choose you
for sure.'

Ben studies my face for a moment, but doesn't
say anything. Then he gets up off the bench. He
shoots me a tight smile. 'We'd better get you back to
school,' is all he says.

# Thursday 10 July

## 5 p.m.

The rest of the afternoon passes by in a blur, 'cos everyone's freaking out about this presentation. Even Mr Reeve's super-stressed 'cos he yells at Meadow Jenkins for asking one too many questions about genealogy and Meadow Jenkins doesn't get yelled at for *anything*. Then the bell goes and while the rest of the school heads home, we have to stay and get ready 'cos the presentation starts at 5 p.m.

The whole time I'm sitting at Jupiter table, not saying anything to anyone, and this sinking feeling in my stomach grows and grows. It's like I've got a lump of lead bundled up in a cloth and there's a ball and chain weighing it down, down, down. 'Cos all anyone can bang on about is how brilliant their family is and how they're all coming to see this flaming presentation. Just at Jupiter table, it's all:

Rashid: 'My great-grandmother has six fingers on her left hand.'

Jemima: 'We've not officially confirmed we're related to Kate Middleton but my dad's dentist once saw Prince Andrew at a boat show.'

Stacy: 'I can say the alphabet backwards in 3.47 seconds. Mum taught me. She can't wait for me to show it off tonight.'

This lump in my stomach is 'cos everyone else's family is going to be here, but mine won't bother, 'cos they all properly hate me now. Why would they? They sent Ben to take me to my appointment with Jess – like heck Mum and Dad were busy. And I know – I just *know* – Ben's told them about his football match by now. He'd have been straight on his mobile after our little 'chat' in the park. Dad's bound to choose that, isn't he? Mum and Dad can barely look at me when they talk to me at home –

why would they want to sit in my school hall and look at me on stage when they can go and watch Ben be all brilliant in the park?

Before we know it, Miss Watson's popping her head round the door and saying, 'Mr Reeve? Time to get them lined up,' and we're all filing out into the school hall.

Some parents are already there, and Stacy points and waves at her mum and little sister as we troop in. There's a posh woman who looks a bit like a horse and Jemima waves as we pass by. Rashid's mum, dad and sisters are sat there, along with an old woman I think might be his gran, or his great-gran, but I can't see how many fingers she has.

No sign of my parents.

As we troop up the stairs to the stage, I spot Frankie Mellor in the third row, next to her mum and dad. Her face turns a bright shade of pink as I catch her eye and she stares down at the ground. We merge with 5W and sit on the benches that have been placed on the stage. Everyone's clutching their notes. Meadow Jenkins carries a huge piece of cardboard under her arm. Somehow I get sat next to Samir Stamford, on the bench right in front of Murphy. I can feel Murphy's eyes burning into the back of my head but I make sure I don't turn round to say anything to him. Well, you know what I mean. He's properly annoying me, is Murphy. Saying all those mean things about me. Calling me a Mutant. That's hardly friendship, is it? Friends are meant to be there for you come rain or shine, through thick and thin, whether you want to talk or not, whether you act like an idiot or a champion.

'Your mum and dad coming?' Samir asks, leaning into me.

I scowl and shake my head.

'Mine neither,' Samir says, and the corners of his mouth slope down a bit. 'Mum's got to work and Dad's on holiday with his new girlfriend. Even though Jess told both of them about this. Still, can't be helped.' He forces a little smile. 'What are you going to do for yours?'

I shrug. Samir jerks his thumb behind him. 'They're all taking bets, you know.'

I look at him quizzically. 'Murphy's running a sweepstake,' Samir explains. 'People have put money on whether you're going to mime, or do sign language, or interpretive dance, or actually speak when it's your turn. Though you having a meltdown is the odds-on favourite. Couldn't give me a heads up, could you? I've got a pound on you burping your way through it.'

I can't help myself, and I burst out laughing. Samir joins in for a moment until Mr Reeve crosses the stage and glares at us to be quiet. He takes his place behind the lectern and turns to the audience. All the chairs are taken. There are even parents standing at the back of the hall. The waiter from Pizza Express and the café's one of them. His hair looks a bit whiter since we last saw him, though. I scan the seats for my family one final time.

Nothing.

I can feel hot pricks of tears behind my eyes, 'cos I can't believe it. I mean, as much as I've been worrying about them not turning up, and thinking that they hate me, a small part of me – a teeny, tiny part of me – still kept thinking that they'd show. That somehow, they'd remember how much they *did* love me and they'd turn up to clap me after all.

But I guess not.

I tuck my chin into the collar of my school shirt as Mr Reeve starts welcoming the parents 'cos I don't want anyone to see my eyes are filling with tears.

'. . . worked very hard on this,' Mr Reeve's saying. 'We didn't want Year Six to have all the fun with their leavers' assembly, so the aim of this task is to explore not just one's family tree, but the history and heritage of their ancestry . . .'

My throat's burning and my jaw's aching 'cos I'm trying so hard not to cry. My stomach feels like someone's trying to scoop my guts out with a cheese wire. And one thought's swirling round and round my brain:

THEY DIDN'T COME THEY DIDN'T COME THEY DIDN'T COME THEY DIDN'T COME . . .

I just want to curl up into a ball right here on the stage.

Another thought pops into my head:

THEY CHOSE BEN THEY CHOSE BEN THEY CHOSE BEN THEY CHOSE BEN ...

I feel like a Stinking Bishop wrapped up in a piece of mouldy Stilton, with a thick slab of crusty, out-of-date, flaming stolen Wensleydale on top.

'Sorry! Sorry! Ow, Rob, mind my foot!'

I snap my head up and blink back the tears so I can see. It takes a second and my ears hear them first.

'I think there are some seats over there.'

'Thank you, Jacob lad.'

'No, Lucy, this way.'

And there, at the back of the hall, traipsing in like a circus troupe or a small army, is Mum, looking all flustered, Lucy toddling alongside, Susie stage-whispering so she's actually really loud, Robbie with his guitar strapped to his back and bumping into everyone 'cos he never cuts his fringe, Jacob adjusting his glasses, and Dad, wiping

his big conk of a nose on a 'Swindon Town FC'
handkerchief.

And they're making absolutely the worst racket
possible.

'Oh, excuse me! Sorry! Excuse me!' Dad's going.
Then, 'Oh, hey, you're from that café the other day!
Ooh, sorry, was that your foot?'

'Yoooooooooooowwwwwwwww!' the Pizza
Express waiter cries out in pain. There's a flurry
of movement and then he staggers out of the hall
doors, like we're the worst thing that's ever happened
to him.

Mum spots me up on stage. 'Anthony!' she trills.
'Sorry we're late. Problem with the people carrier.'
She smiles as Mrs Wintour gets up from the front
row and ushers them into the seats there.

Crikey. They take up THE ENTIRE ROW!

Still. I'm breaming a SEA BREAM kind of a
smile. They're here. Holy Moly! They do love me
after all!

On stage, Mr Reeve looks a bit shell-shocked,
which is what some soldiers in the First World

War were, what with all the banging and noise and bombs exploding. This commotion's not far off, truth be told. 'Uh,' he's going. 'Let's crack on, shall we?' He turns to the first pupil on the bench. It's Lee Foreman, and he nearly trips over his feet as he gets up, clutching his piece of paper in his hands, shaking with nerves.

'In 1914, my great-granny Ida was born,' Lee's going, his teeth chattering, 'and she once told Hitler to bog off . . .'

I zone him out 'cos I want to think a minute. Something's not quite right. Something's really niggling me, like I've got an itch on my very brain and I'm not sure what's going to soothe it. 'Cos even though I'm so happy – I'm *ecstatic* – that my family turned up, the knot in my stomach still feels like it's the size of Wiltshire.

The audience applauds as Lee takes his bow and returns to his seat. Samir gets up and heads to the front of the stage. And he takes his page of notes and folds it into four, and then puts it in his pocket. 'I'm sorry, Miss Watson,' he says and looks to where she's sat next to Mr Reeve on the stage, 'but there's no point doing this. My parents aren't here to see it, and I'm sure no one else is fussed about my family tree.'

Mr Reeve splutters to say something, but Miss Watson puts her hand on his arm to stop him. That perks him up no end. 'Don't worry, Mr Reeve, I don't mind,' Samir says. 'And Woody Wattler hasn't got anything he'd like to say, either.'

In the front row, I catch Mum wiping her eyes with a tissue. I don't know what she's got to be sad about – she hardly knows Samir. Samir sits back down, aware that the whole school are looking at him. He shrugs at me, then gestures to the front of the stage.

'Anthony!' Mr Reeve leans forward in his seat. 'You're up.'

Behind me, Murphy, Michael Hadley and a couple of girls from 5W break into giggles. Murphy rubs his hands together. 'A fiver on him going nuts,' he whispers.

I huff and slowly get up from my seat. My legs

feel all shaky, and I stumble over to the side of the stage. 'Anthony!' Mr Reeve hisses at me. 'Where are you going?'

I hold up my hand as if to say 'Chill out', and pick up the piece of cardboard and Mum's cool box I'd asked Mrs Wintour to leave there. I totter over to the front of the stage and peer down to see Mum, Dad, Susie, Jacob, Robbie and Lucy look up at me expectantly. Here goes.

I hold up the piece of cardboard for people to see, and everyone leans forward in their seats to peer at it. I've amended it slightly, so as well as the pie-chart circle and the 'Three of my family have blond hair. Three have brown, though Dad's going bald. One is a redhead' comment, it also reads:

The redhead is Susie. But that doesn't make her any less part of the family. She's just got hair a different colour, that's all. She's still a Button.

Susie goes to leap up from her seat to run on stage and give me a hug but Dad restrains her. Instead, she yells, 'Oh, Anthony!' and looks like someone's just told her she's won *The Voice*.

But it *still* doesn't feel right.

There's a smattering of applause and everyone quietens down to see what I'll do next.

I place Jacob's pie chart on the floor and open the cool box. From it, I take out the wheel of cheese and everyone gasps as I present it to the crowd.

'Cos it's not just a wheel of cheese any more. I discovered last night that if I kept chipping and chipping away at the Cheddar, it would mould and crumble into whatever shape I wanted. So not only does the cheese now properly look like number 12 Conway Avenue, I took some of Lucy's Lego pieces and placed them around the wheel. Mum and Dad are in the 'garden', Jacob's hanging out of the first-floor window, Lucy is in one of the bedrooms, Susie's in the bathroom and Robbie's in the converted garage. Except I ran out of Lego pieces, so Robbie's represented here by a Darth Vader figurine, but he doesn't look like he minds too much.

The audience clap loudly in appreciation and I

look to see even Mr Reeve with a huge smile of wonder on his face.

I nod my head at the crowd to say 'thanks' but I still can't help feeling a bit glum. I place the wheel of cheese back in the cool box, but as I'm zipping it shut I notice something stuffed down in the corner.

I reach in and take out a screwed-up piece of paper. I open it to read:

## BUT I *LIKE* CAMPING IN CORNWALL

Of course. I'd shoved it in there the other day, after the picnic in the park that Sunday, when I didn't want anyone knowing that I had written the exact same thing that Ben had said. 'Cos I didn't want anyone to think how alike we were, like we were related or something.

And as I'm reading the piece of paper, and thinking about Ben, my stomach keeps churning over and over, like how people churn cheese. I look out into the audience, and see Mum, Dad, Robbie,

Susie, Jacob and Lucy all smiling at me. I think back to what Ben said in the park earlier. About how it's always been just him and his mum, all his life.

My mind flashes back to the quote hanging on Jess's wall:

> *At the core of ethics: a command that one try to imagine what it might be like to be someone else.*
> *Alain de Botton*

I mean, all right, Ben probably hasn't got to queue for the bathroom, or have to wear hand-me-downs from his older brother, or to only get five minutes at a time on the Xbox.

But still. How boring.

I know my stomach's churning like Cheddar 'cos there's one more Lego man – or *Star Wars* figurine – missing. He's at his football match. The match *I* didn't want Dad to go to 'cos I thought he would think Ben was better than me and was worth spending more time with than me. But that's not true, is it? Dad and Mum and Susie and Robbie and

Jacob and Lucy are here, after all. After all the mean things I've written and said and thought and done over the past few days, they still came.

'Wait!' I suddenly cry. 'Ben!'

And the whole hall gasps as my words ring out. Mum clutches Dad's hand.

'Yes!!' someone hisses behind me, and coins jingle in pockets. In the second row, I see Mrs Wintour handing over a tenner to the lady next to her.

My whole family and Mr Reeve and Miss Watson and Samir and Murphy and Stacy and Michael Hadley and EVERYONE are leaning forwards in their chairs to see what I'm going to say next.

'The boy speaks!' a man at the back of the hall says, and Mum turns round to glare at him.

And just there, at the back of the audience, my eye catches something shining in the evening sun. A chink of bright light bounces off the back wall. It's from a shiny, posh silver watch on somebody's wrist.

The knot in my stomach evaporates as Ben steps forward from the back of the audience. 'Yes?'

I point at him. 'You came?'

He nods shyly. 'Wouldn't miss it for the world.'

'Over here,' Dad shouts to him, and Ben makes his way down the aisle and slides in at the end of the row next to Susie.

Hang on a second, that's not right.

'Go on, Ant,' Dad soothes.

I take a deep breath. 'Ben shouldn't be here,' I say.

Ben's shoulders slump when he hears that. Mum bites her lip, and looks at me in disappointment. Dad's eyebrows knit together. 'Anthony,' he warns, 'we've talked about this.'

'No!' I say. 'Wait! Ben *shouldn't* be here.'

Dad jumps up and looks like he's going to come up on stage and throttle me. 'Ben is your family,' Dad thunders, 'whether you like it or not. I know it hasn't been easy, it's been a shock to everyone, but we're just going to have to get on with it.'

Mr Reeve stands up. 'Uh, Mr Button,' he says, 'if you'd prefer to do this in private . . .'

'I didn't mean that,' I say. 'I know Ben's family

now. I—' I can't quite find the right words. My voice sounds all shaky. 'At first I was really angry he just showed up out of nowhere and strolled into our family like he had every right to be there. 'Cos I thought he was just one more person to compete with. One more person to have to share your and Mum's love with.'

Mum looks to Dad then like her heart's just broken. 'Anthony,' she says, but I hold up my hand to stop her.

'But I know it's not like that,' I continue. 'I know that I'm really lucky to have a family at all. Samir's not got one. Not really. Sorry, Sam,' I say, turning to him. He shrugs his shoulders in agreement.

'And I know family *isn't* a competition. It's not about all of us having to compete for your love. I know you love us all equally, right?'

Dad and Mum nod in unison. 'Of course we do,' Dad says, and then he sighs. 'I didn't realize you felt this way. I mean, I thought your not talking was probably something to do with Ben turning up out of the blue, but perhaps we could have been more supportive of such a big change. I'm sorry.'

'That's OK. I get it now. But sometimes it's really hard to say the things that you're feeling. Especially to the people closest to you. Sometimes we don't tell each other what we really want to say, 'cos we're scared and embarrassed, or we don't want to get our feelings hurt. So we don't say anything. Like me.'

Mum and Dad nod slowly, a glimmer of understanding on their faces.

'Like Susie,' I continue. 'She doesn't like it when we make fun of her having red hair while none of us do apart from the milkman.'

A few parents at the back of the hall giggle at that, though I don't know why.

'Like Jacob,' I plough on. 'He feels different to all of us 'cos he's so brainy and thinks we think he's weird and geeky.'

Mum looks to Jacob with tears in her eyes. 'Is that true?'

Jacob looks at her shyly. 'Sometimes,' he whispers, and Mum lets out this little whimper.

'Like Mr Reeve,' I continue.

Mr Reeve looks at me like I've grown another head. 'Excuse me?'

'It's so obvious you fancy Miss Watson, but you can't tell her,' I say, and every single pupil giggles and goes, 'Ooooo-ooooo.' Mr Reeve goes bright red, but Miss Watson places her hand on his arm again and they share a smile.

'It's true,' Mr Reeve whispers, and Miss Watson beams from ear to ear. At the back of the hall, Mr Farah's looking none too pleased, but you can't have everything.

'Like Frankie Mellor,' I say, and Frankie goes as red as a medieval fire engine when I say her name. 'She can't speak and say the things she wants to, and I know she gets so frustrated.'

Jessica Mellor, her little sister, and the smallest girl in Year 5, stands up behind me. 'Not yet, she can't,' Jessica says, 'but I know she'll cure it one day.'

Frankie beams up at her, which is nice. It must be nice having your family say nice things about you, mustn't it? Least I flaming well hope it is, else I'm stuffed.

I gaze around the hall, trying to think of more examples. 'Like – like—'

A woman stands up in the middle of the third row. 'Like,' she says, her voice barely above a whisper, 'like I'm a secret lemonade drinker,' she mutters.

Her husband's eyebrows shoot upwards. 'What about your diet?' he cries.

She shrugs, then slumps back down.

'Like, I love listening to gangsta rap,' one old woman yells.

'Like, I'm secretly addicted to *Homes under the Hammer*!'

'Like, I eat peanut-butter sandwiches in bed!'

'Like, I really hate going to Swindon matches!' one woman cries, 'but I have to because my husband's fanatical about them.'

Her husband looks at her in wonder. 'I only go because I thought *you* liked them,' he laughs.

'Like,' Michael Hadley says loudly, jumping to his feet, 'like I've got two mums!'

Everyone turns to look at him. 'What?' I cry.

Michael shrugs. 'My real mum and then Karen,

Mum's partner.' He looks down at his presentation notes. 'That's a spoiler alert, by the way.'

Some of the pupils on the back benches properly snigger at him, but Stacy and Rashid shoot them filthy looks to shut them up.

'Like, I hate it, absolutely hate it when my mother-in-law comes to stay,' one man cries.

'Like, I like wearing high heels!' cries another man.

Everyone starts giggling away, and I nod enthusiastically. 'Right. All of those things. And I suppose the *real* reason I didn't speak for so long was because I thought that was "my thing". I thought I had to have a *thing* to belong in my family. What with Jacob being so brainy, and Susie being so good at acting, and Robbie being really good at guitar. I wasn't really good at anything, really, apart from knowing about cheese. So I kept on not talking, 'cos I thought that was all I was good at.'

I think back to Jess's words. And Mum's.

'But now I know I can be anything I want to be – it's just that I might not have figured out exactly what that is yet.'

People are staring at me in confusion now. I'm sort of winging this bit, truth be told. I'm fully aware everyone must think I'm the world's biggest purple beard-o, and I can't think of anything else to say to get my point across.

Except –

The lyrics of 'Hall of Fame' spring to mind. I guess that's what happens when you're forced to listen to it over and over again, and I begin to chant the verses out loud. After all, who *wouldn't* want to be in a hall of fame, be the best, be a champion? People are looking at me like I'm *absolutely* the most purple beard-o thing they've ever seen.

'Um,' I plough on, building to the chorus, to the bit Robbie kept on getting wrong. But my voice sort of peters out at the end of the last sentence. This is probably the most excruciating, embarrassing thing ever to happen to me. I know my cheeks are as red as anything.

All of a sudden, Robbie grabs his guitar and leaps up on stage next to me. Susie's not far behind. Together they belt out the lyrics with gusto and suddenly we are all singing our hearts out, just like we did the other day doing the washing-up.

Except this time, three hundred pairs of eyes are staring at us.

Just as I'm thinking how much I wish I'd never started this flaming song, behind me Stacy, Rashid, Jemima and Samir get up from their seats and start singing along too. And then Jessica Mellor, then Amy Mason and Lauren Allen, then Lee Foreman and then Michael Hadley and Constance Ngoru stand up, and we're all singing the words loud and clear.

It's a Year 5 chorus – and I reckon The Script, and even will.i.am, would be proud of the way we're sounding so good. Heck, we *deserve* to be in anyone's hall of fame after this!

At the end of the song, there's a smattering of applause and Robbie and Susie head back to their seats, while the brave souls in Year 5 who stood up to sing with me sit back down on the benches.

Murphy sniggers at me, but I can't help smiling, though, 'cos I reckon all those people who stood up are *truly* my friends, not like Murphy. How lucky am I to have such good friends who are willing to look like idiots with me!

Mr Reeve leaps up from his seat. 'Excellent stuff, Anthony,' he says. 'Very imaginative. And an excellent way to sum up what I'm always saying – dare to dream big! No limits to your imagination! Don't just be a passenger on the bus of life, kids. Be the driver!' He thinks for a moment. 'Not to say I'm telling you all to go out and be bus drivers. I mean, you can if you want. It's a perfectly noble occupation. What I'm saying is, don't just drift through life. If you really take charge, as Anthony says, you could be anything!'

'It's The Script saying it, really,' I point out. 'And will.i.am.'

'Very good.' Mr Reeve nods and ploughs on. 'Right. Next up is . . .'

But just then my eye catches Ben's and I remember why I started going on about this whole thing in the first place. 'Ben's really good at football!' I yell, and even Mr Reeve stops banging on and turns to look at me. 'Like, *really* good. And I was trying to tell you why Ben *shouldn't* be here.'

Everyone quietens down to hear me out. ''Cos it's the tenth,' I add.

Dad looks from me to Ben. 'And?'

Ben shifts uncomfortably in his chair. 'Don't worry about it, Anthony,' he mumbles.

'But I do!' I cry. 'I've been so nasty to you this whole time and now I've got the chance to make it up to you. You shouldn't be here, 'cos you should be at Furton Park playing football 'cos you've got a talent scout from Reading coming down to see if you can play for them.'

Everyone turns to Ben, shocked. I hope the hall floor's clean 'cos Dad's jaw is practically living there.

'A talent scout?' someone whispers. 'In Furton Yarrow?'

'Is that so?' Dad says.

Ben lets out a sigh, then nods. 'But I'd rather be here,' he says, and something about his face tells me he really means that too.

'Well, stuff that!' I shout.

'Anthony!' Mum, Dad and Mr Reeve cry in unison.

'Sorry,' I mumble, and I take a flying leap off the stage. 'But we've got to get to Furton Park before it's too late!' I land on the floor and race to the hall doors.

'Uh,' Mr Reeve stutters as the hall breaks out into chatter and excitement and a smattering of applause. 'The presentation!'

Samir leaps up from his seat, followed by Michael Hadley, Lee Foreman and half of the second row. 'Stuff that!' Samir shouts.

'Samir!' Mr Reeve cries.

'That was Woody Wattler,' Samir retorts, leaping off the stage.

And then it's pandemonium. All the parents get up from their chairs and head towards the hall doors, just as all the pupils leap off the stage to join them.

'Ah!' Mr Reeve's yelling. 'Come back! 5R, where do you think you're going? Meadow Jenkins! I expected better of *you*.'

'I'm sorry, Mr Reeve,' Meadow shouts over her shoulder as she storms towards the exit, trampling over her presentation cardboard as she goes, 'but we're talking about a talent scout! Nothing that exciting ever happens in Furton Yarrow!'

Miss Watson slides her arm through Mr Reeve's. 'Come on, Christopher,' she says. 'You know you'd love to see it.' Mr Reeve's name is Christopher! Holy Moly!

Mr Reeve lets out a sigh. 'If you can't beat 'em,' he smiles, and he leaps off the stage to join the rest of the parents and pupils trickling through the hall doors.

# Thursday 10 July

## 6 p.m.

I've never seen Furton Yarrow Park so busy. The car ride to get here passed by in a blur, 'cos Dad put his foot down and Mum kept yelling, 'It's only forty,' and Ben was saying, 'I really don't mind,' and Robbie was going, 'Don't be stupid, you have to try out,' and Jacob was saying, 'I can't believe you didn't tell us there's going to be a talent scout,' and I was saying, 'He told me, but I didn't tell anyone,' and Susie was saying, 'OMG, Anthony totally talked. He's such a drama queen, but like, in a really good way,' and Lucy was going, 'Boots! Boots!' 'cos she was playing *Dora the Explorer* on her DS.

I kept looking out the back window to see about a million cars following us in a convoy, all intent on getting to the park to see Ben and this talent scout.

It's crowded when we get there, and everyone's hogging the sidelines but we manage to get to the front of the crowd 'cos Mum rams the buggy at people's ankles. Ben goes off to get changed into his kit while Dad shakes the talent scout man's hand. He's got a bigger nose than Dad, this talent scout man, so I reckon they're going to hit it off. 'Cutting it a bit fine, aren't you?' the man says, but Dad starts jabbering on about problems with the people carrier.

Then Ben and all his teammates traipse onto the pitch and everyone from my school and everyone watching on the sidelines cheers him on. I'm wearing Dad's Swindon scarf and the crowd's a sea of red and white scarves and banners. It's like Saturday afternoon at The County Ground.

As Ben and his mates warm up and start kicking the ball about between them, I spot a woman hovering nervously at the side of the pitch. She's tall and has her brown hair pulled back into a bun. She's wringing her hands nervously. I tug Dad's sleeve. 'Dad? Is that . . . ?'

Dad follows my gaze and spots the woman. He smiles awkwardly. 'Yep,' he says. 'Best go and say hello.' And he wanders off to speak to the woman.

Mum looks over at the pair of them, noting their awkward conversation. 'That's Ben's mum, isn't it?' I ask. Mum nods.

Then the referee blows the whistle and the game kicks off. Right there at the front of the crowd, whooping away, is Mr Reeve. He looks over to me. 'Not a bad family trait, potentially playing for England,' he laughs.

'Steady on!' I frown, but that just makes Mr Reeve laugh even more. 'You know, Mr Reeve,' I say, 'you're not a bad teacher, you know.'

Mr Reeve acts like he's ecstatic. 'Well, that's praise indeed coming from you,' he grins. 'Does this mean you won't be making squelching noises at me while my back's turned from now on?'

I grin up at him. Then I spot Murphy in amongst

the crowd, laughing with Michael Hadley and Lee Foreman. Lee waves me over. 'This is really cool, Anthony!' He smiles when I bustle my way through the crowd to them. 'Your bro could be the next Wayne Rooney.'

Murphy doesn't look me in the eye. 'Could I have his autograph?' he mumbles.

I burst out laughing. 'Not likely,' I reply. 'He doesn't give autographs to purple beard-os.'

Murphy looks a bit guilty at that. 'I'm sorry I was a bit of an idiot,' he says. 'Calling you names, and all that.'

I shrug. 'Whatever. I've got new mates now.' I nod to where Samir, Rashid, Stacy and Frankie Mellor are chatting in the crowd. 'Mates who don't think I'm a mutant.'

And with that I spin on my heel and head over to my family. I can sense Murphy's properly angry, but I don't care. I don't know why I was ever friends with him, to be honest. He's always getting me into trouble, making me do things I don't want to do, thinking he was properly funny when I just wanted him to like me. I just didn't see it before.

Dad's still chatting to Ben's mum, so I grab Susie, Robbie and Jacob and haul them over to meet her.

'Hello!' I say, breaking into their conversation. She looks down on me in surprise. 'H–hello,' she stutters.

I hold out my hand. 'I'm Anthony. Ben's brother.'

She takes my hand, a bit dazed, truth be told, and shakes it warmly. 'One of them, anyway,' I add, and I turn to Robbie, Jacob and Susie and introduce each of them in turn.

Ben's mum nods. 'Ben's told me all about you.' She smiles. 'I could have guessed who you all were.' She peers over to the other side of the pitch and gives Mum and Lucy a little smile. Mum and Lucy wave back.

Dad pats me on the back. 'Come on then,' he says, and we head back to Mum. 'That was very mature of you,' Dad whispers to me. He takes Lucy from the buggy and hoists her onto his shoulders. 'Like cheese.'

From the corner of my eye, I catch Jacob gazing up into the sky, probably thinking about Jupiter aligning with Mars.

'Wait!' I cry, and all my family turn to look at me. Well, all my family except Ben, obviously, 'cos he's too busy passing to the guy in midfield. 'We can't go to Disneyland Paris!'

'Why not?' Robbie frowns. 'I thought the whole point of you not talking was so we could get a decent holiday.'

I shake my head. 'Not really. I wasn't talking 'cos it was my way of making people pay attention to me when everyone was paying attention to Ben and saying how brilliant he is and isn't it wonderful we've got another wonderful brother in our lives.'

Dad narrows his eyes at me. 'Where's this going?'

'We can't go to Disneyland Paris,' I repeat, ''cos we have to send Jacob to space camp.'

Jacob looks at me, his eyes wide, while everyone else mutters their confusion. 'What are you talking about?' Mum asks.

'Jacob?' I say, and nod at him to tell all.

Jacob gulps. 'My school wants to send me to space camp,' he says nervously. 'But it doesn't matter.'

'Oh, for goodness' sake,' I cry. 'His school are sending him and four other people only, 'cos Jacob's one of the best and is brilliant at space and they want him to go to NASA. NASA! That's practically the moon! But they can't pay for all of it so every family has to pay a few hundred pounds and we can't pay that and go to Disneyland Paris.'

Everyone looks at Jacob in wonder. Mum shakes her head in disbelief. 'Why didn't you say anything?'

Jacob looks at me. I can see he doesn't want to get me in trouble. I sigh. ''Cos I told him not to. I said, don't tell Mum and Dad 'cos they'll just be upset they can't afford to send you there *and* take us on holiday, when really I wanted to go on holiday and I was annoyed that Jacob was brilliant at something and I wasn't. I was just being selfish. Sorry.'

Robbie and Susie whisper to each other. Susie nods. 'We don't mind,' she says, a hint of theatricality in her voice, like she's sacrificing herself for the greater good. 'We'll not go on holiday if it means Jacob can go to space camp.'

Dad beams at them, then looks at me. 'You happy with that?'

I nod. 'Jess says I have stamina and willpower like no one else she's ever met and she bets I could put it to good use. So I don't mind not going on holiday, 'cos I'm going to take up cheese carving. I quite enjoyed that.'

Mum and Dad burst out laughing. 'That sounds like a plan,' Dad says. 'Well, then. That's settled.'

Jacob can't believe his ears. Mum ruffles his hair. 'I'm sure we can work something out,' she says. 'We'll get you to space, don't worry. And maybe, *maybe*, we could stretch to camping in Cornwall after all.'

Susie mulls this over. 'Kate Moss *does* go glamping,' she says. 'Yes. Yes, that could work.'

'And Robbie's got his guitar,' Dad says. 'So that's the campfire sorted.'

I groan. 'As long as he learns another song.'

Robbie grins. 'Fair point,' he says.

Jacob's eyes fill with tears and he takes a Swindon

Town FC handkerchief from his pocket. 'Th-thank you,' he snuffles, looking at all of us like his heart is going to burst. 'Thank you. I – I can't believe it.'

Dad hoicks Lucy down to the floor and leans over and gives Jacob a hug. Just as we're being all soppy and family-y, the crowd lets out an almighty cheer and we turn just in time to see Ben chip the ball into the net.

'GOAL!!!!!' Dad cries, leaping up and down and we all get squashed and jostled as everyone in the crowd around us starts jumping for joy. 'COME ON, MY SON!!!!'

Dad kisses Mum on the top of her head. Robbie picks Susie up and twirls her round and she's working the crowd like she's just won the Oscar for Best Actress.

On the other side of the pitch, the talent scout is deep in conversation with Ben's mum and they're shaking hands. I've got a good feeling about this.

I hang back a little bit and take it all in.

My brilliant brother, off to space camp to be the next Neil Armstrong.

My fabulous sister, one day set to take Hollywood by storm.

My wonderful elder brother, going on to be a rock star.

My cute little sister, who can say more words than any other two-year-old I know. Even though I don't know any other two-year-olds.

And my Steven Gerrard–like brother scoring a goal in front of a talent scout!

Dad slings his arms round my shoulders. 'Fancy Pizza Express tonight? My treat.'

I shrug. If I'm honest, I've still not *properly* forgiven them for going on about my Padana last time.

'You wouldn't say no to a cheese pizza, would you?' Mum smiles.

'Goat's cheese *and* Mozzarella?' Jacob says. 'It'll be *dairy* good.'

'That's *my* joke!' I protest.

'Calm down, Man . . . chego!' Robbie laughs.

Dad booms. 'My cheese jokes are Feta than that!'

Mum rolls her eyes. 'Not this again.'

'Don't Roquefort the boat!' Susie trills.

They all look at me, their eyes sparkling with glee. When I don't say anything for about ten seconds, panic flashes across Mum's face. 'Oh, Anthony,' she whispers. Clearly she thinks I'm going to stop talking again.

I take a deep breath and say, 'Is that all you've got? That's all the cheese you can name, isn't it?'

And everyone looks at me like I'm a bit purple beard-o, but I don't mind. ''Cos the one thing I can do,' I continue, 'well, the one thing I can do *as well* as stop talking longer than most people, is cheese. I can name over four hundred and three different varieties of cheese. We have the Muenster, the Provolone, Caerphilly, Shropshire Blue, which is actually orange, Brie . . .'

Dad groans. 'Oh, God. I think I preferred it when you *didn't* talk.' Mum wallops him. 'Kidding!' he yells. And he leans in to hug me.

Then Mum hugs me on top of Dad. Then Susie, then Robbie, then Jacob, then Lucy, and all the time I'm going, 'Camembert, Beaufort, like the wind scale, and it *does* give you wind, Flosserkäse,

Ribiola . . .' except some of it's a bit muffled 'cos my face is in Dad's belly button. His *Buttony* button . . .

And apart from that, apart from all the soppy hugging and being nice to each other like we've not really done before, and them going on and on and on about my obsession with cheese, life's not too bad, really. All in all. Truth be told.

# Acknowledgements

This book couldn't have existed without the input of a lot of brilliant people. And also the input of a lot of cheese into my digestive system, but that was all in the name of research, you understand.

A massive thank you to everyone at Random House Children's Publishers for their support and skill, particularly Natalie Doherty for her feedback in the early stages, Jasmine Joynson, and Carmen McCullough. Thank you to Sue Cook, whose copyediting skills are the best, bar none. Most of all, a HUGE, GINORMOUS, SPECTACULAR thank you to the best editor in town (it's a small town) Becky Stradwick. Thanks, Bek, for your enthusiasm, feedback, and all-round good-egg-ed-ness.

Thank you to United Agents, particuarly the encouragement and expertise of agent extraordinaire Jodie Hodges (yes, that one) and Julian Dickson.

Thanks to the incomparable Tony Ross for his brilliant illustration. I feel very privileged it's adorning this book.

Thanks to Claire and Chris Duguid for answering my questions about Child Psychology. Thanks to Matt Arnold for answering my questions about Swindon Town FC (after repeated badgering).

Thanks to the barista at Costa who not only served me, but didn't eject me from the premises or look at me like I was a purple beard-o that time I popped in for a coffee and had to write everything down with a notepad and pen because I was researching what it was like to not talk for a day. Thanks also for laughing at my 'Thanks a Latte' comment. It was a pity laugh, but I'll take it.

Thank you to my friends for their encouragement and support. And by 'encouragement' and 'support', I mean, 'continuing to mock me 28 years later for having had speech therapy as a child and basically comparing my childhood to *The King's Speech*'.

And lastly, thanks to my family for their continued support – Mum, Dad, Andrew – and Charlotte, who's actually read the books – and now Lily, too. What a marvellous bunch of people you are.

Loudest burp?
Freckliest face?
Fastest time to superglue
hand to head?

Luke loves world records. He knows everything
about them – the hairiest man alive, the woman
with the most tattoos, even the world's
most venomous snake.

When Luke finds out his tiny village is going to
be bulldozed to the ground, he concocts a brilliant
plan to make Port Bren famous – by getting
the eccentric villagers to break fifty world records.
In a week.

The clock is ticking.
And the records just keep getting crazier . . .

Dear Your Majesty,

My name is Billie Templar. I live in Merchant Stanton, which is all right, but it's not as nice as Buckingham Palace, I bet. Anyway, I know you're really busy, what with being Queen, but I have a favour to ask you.

Please can you send my dad home from the war? He's been out there for the last eleven weeks. His best friend got blown up today, and I don't want him to get hurt, so please can you excuse him from the fighting?

Billie

'Sweet, funny, heartbreaking, and
massively feel-good . . . a real must-read'
*The Bookbag*

Join Pea on her BIG MOVE TO LONDON

and her quest to find a new best friend.

(Which is harder than it sounds . . .)

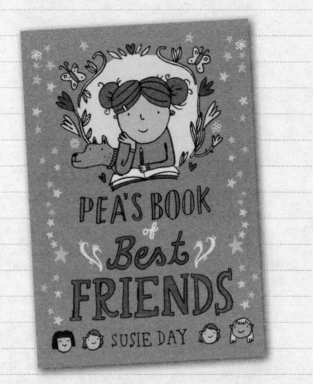

Warning! This book is not about mermaids.

# MEET
# DARCY BURDOCK

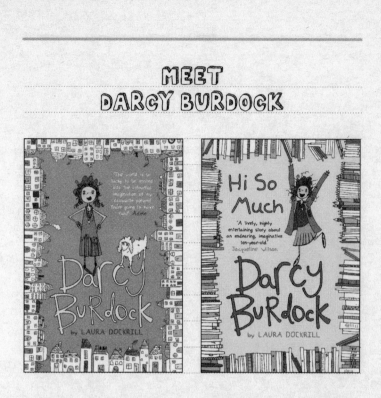

'A lively, highly entertaining story about an
endearing, imaginative ten-year-old'
*Jacqueline Wilson*

'Everyone's falling for Laura Dockrill'
*VOGUE*